P9-CFE-645

Why had she taken a year's sabbatical? Jenna hadn't said a word about having children of her own.

Maybe she'd had a child, then lost it.

Lorenzo knew how that felt, and he didn't talk about it. He could understand why someone just wouldn't want the constant reminder of the empty spaces in their lives. Besides, she'd hit the nail on the head about his own situation.

"Very true," he said. "Life can be unexpected." And sometimes it took you a while to pick yourself up and dust yourself off again. "If you want anyone to test you on stuff before the exams, give me a yell."

"Thanks. That's kind." She smiled at him, and he had to tamp down the urge to lace his fingers through hers and suggest something more personal than revision.

This was ridiculous. They'd both said that they weren't in the market for a relationship.

Yet something about Jenna Harris drew him. Her warmth, her verve, her kindness.

He was going to have to be careful about this. Really careful.

Dear Reader,

When my editor asked me for an Italian hero, I knew exactly where I needed to set part of the book—Verona, where my husband and I had just celebrated our twenty-fifth wedding anniversary!

Lorenzo and Jenna's story is all about family. About the greatest gift you can give anyone, and the most heart-wrenching loss. Both of them picked the wrong partner the last time around, and neither wanted to risk their heart again—until they met each other.

Their journey's about learning to move on, put the past behind them and dare to risk opening their hearts again. I hope you enjoy the story—and the glimpse of Verona!

With love,

Kate Hardy

UNLOCKING THE ITALIAN DOC'S HEART

KATE HARDY

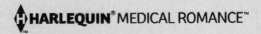

If you purchased this book without a cover you should be aware that this book is stolen property. It was reported as "unsold and destroyed" to the publisher, and neither the author nor the publisher has received any payment for this "stripped book."

Recycling programs
for this product may
not exist in your area.

ISBN-13: 978-1-335-66356-6

Unlocking the Italian Doc's Heart

First North American Publication 2018

Copyright © 2018 by Pamela Brooks

All rights reserved. Except for use in any review, the reproduction or utilization of this work in whole or in part in any form by any electronic, mechanical or other means, now known or hereafter invented, including xerography, photocopying and recording, or in any information storage or retrieval system, is forbidden without the written permission of the publisher, Harlequin Enterprises Limited, 22 Adelaide St. West, 40th Floor, Toronto, Ontario M5H 4E3, Canada.

This is a work of fiction. Names, characters, places and incidents are either the product of the author's imagination or are used fictitiously, and any resemblance to actual persons, living or dead, business establishments, events or locales is entirely coincidental.

This edition published by arrangement with Harlequin Books S.A.

For questions and comments about the quality of this book, please contact us at CustomerService@Harlequin.com.

® and TM are trademarks of Harlequin Enterprises Limited or its corporate affiliates. Trademarks indicated with ® are registered in the United States Patent and Trademark Office, the Canadian Intellectual Property Office and in other countries.

Printed in U.S.A.

Books by Kate Hardy

Harlequin Medical Romance

Miracles at Muswell Hill Hospital

Christmas with Her Daredevil Doc
Their Pregnancy Gift

Paddington Children's Hospital

Mommy, Nurse…Duchess?

Christmas Miracles in Maternity

The Midwife's Pregnancy Miracle

Her Playboy's Proposal
Capturing the Single Dad's Heart

Harlequin Romance

Falling for the Secret Millionaire
Her Festive Doorstep Baby
His Shy Cinderella
The Runaway Bride and the Billionaire
Christmas Bride for the Boss

Visit the Author Profile page
at Harlequin.com for more titles.

To my much-loved editor Sheila, with especial thanks for her patience. xx

**Praise for
Kate Hardy**

"Kate Hardy once again brings an entertaining story which will hook readers and keep their interest riveted. The fun banter and witty dialogue makes this a fun read. And the drama in the medical scenes captures the readers' imagination."
—*Goodreads* on *The Midwife's Pregnancy Miracle*

CHAPTER ONE

'JENNA HARRIS—JUST the person I was looking for.' Robert Jones, the head of paediatrics, walked over to Jenna with a man she'd never seen before. 'Jenna, this is Lorenzo Conti, our new senior registrar. He's rostered on to the Paediatric Assessment Unit with you today, so I wondered if you'd mind settling him in?'

'Sure,' Jenna said. She held out her hand to Lorenzo. 'Welcome to the children's department at Muswell Hill Memorial Hospital, Dr Conti.'

'Thank you, Dr Harris,' he said, smiling back. His handshake was firm without being over-pushy, Jenna noticed; she liked that. 'Call me Renzo.'

His voice, with that slight Italian accent, was like melted chocolate. Add those expressive dark eyes, hair that flopped slightly over his forehead and that killer smile, and he'd have all the women in the hospital falling at his feet. And Jenna was horribly aware that her skin was tingling where he was touching her.

Oh, for pity's sake. This was totally inappropriate. Lorenzo Conti was her new colleague. She'd only just met him and he might already be involved with someone. Even if he wasn't, Jenna had promised herself that she was going to focus on her career and make up the ground she'd lost when she'd taken a year's career break. Right now, she really wasn't interested in starting a relationship with anyone; Danny's refusal to support her decision and the ultimatum he'd given her had put her off the idea of sharing her life with anyone else. Ever.

Though she didn't regret the choice she'd made. If she could go back to that moment, knowing what she did now, she'd still make exactly that same choice. The only thing she regretted was her poor judgement. How had she not seen Danny for what he was, earlier? How had she let herself be blinded by all that charm?

'Renzo,' she said, ignoring the fact she felt very slightly flustered. 'I'm Jenna.'

'Jenna,' he said, inclining his head slightly.

She was pretty sure the temperature in the room hadn't suddenly increased by five degrees, though it felt like it.

Oh, honestly. She needed to pull herself together. Now. Be professional, capable and polite, the way she'd normally be with a new member of the team. This pull of attraction towards Lorenzo Conti was something she'd just have to ignore, because it was going nowhere.

'Shall we?' She gestured to the door, and he released her hand.

'In the PAU, we see children who've been referred to us by their family doctor or by the Emergency Department,' she explained as she ushered him through to the assessment area.

'We had a similar system when I worked at the London Victoria,' he said.

'So coming here to Muswell Hill is a promotion for you?' she asked.

'Something like that.'

Though that clearly wasn't the whole story, because it was as if the shutters had just gone down behind his eyes. Whatever had just made him back away from her was none of her business. Time to back off. She smiled and said, 'Let me introduce you to Laney, our triage nurse in the PAU this morning. Laney, this is Dr Conti, our new senior reg.'

'Call me Renzo,' he said, shaking Laney's hand, and Jenna felt ever so slightly better that Laney seemed to be just as flustered by Lorenzo Conti as she'd been.

Their first case was a little girl who'd been eating an orange and stuffed a pip up her nose.

'OK for me to take this one, Renzo?' Jenna asked.

'Sure.'

'Mrs Peters, if you'd like to come this way, I'll examine Callie,' she said with a smile, and ushered the young woman and her daughter through to one of the cubicles.

Renzo could hear Jenna talking, all calm and reassuring with the mum; he liked her bedside manner very much. She was straight-forward, explaining things easily in layman's terms without frightening either the child or the parent, so she'd be good to work with. And he liked what he'd seen of the rest of the team so far. Making a fresh start here at

Muswell Hill Memorial Hospital had definitely been a good idea.

'We see lots of small children who've stuffed something they shouldn't up their nose,' Jenna said, 'and I want to avoid putting Callie through a general anaesthetic and an operation if we can.'

Clearly she'd just looked up Callie's nose with a penlight torch, because then Lorenzo heard her say, 'I can see the pip very clearly, but because it's hard and round I can't put a crocodile clip up Callie's nose to grab it. I can't ask her to blow her nose, either, as she's too little to be able to blow it with the force she'd need to get the pip out, so I'm going to need your help with this. Is that OK?'

'Yes, of course. Just tell me what I need to do,' Mrs Peters said.

'I'm going to lay Callie down on the bed with her head on the pillow and block the nostril that hasn't got the orange pip in it. Then I'm going to ask you to blow into her mouth, and it should make the pip pop straight out. It doesn't always work, and I wouldn't ever advise you to try doing this at home if she does this again,' Jenna warned, 'because it's much safer to do it in hospital where we can act straight away if it doesn't work. But if it does work, that means we don't have to worry about an operation.'

There was a pause while Lorenzo assumed that Jenna was following through the actions she'd just described.

'Yay, it's out!' Jenna said. 'Well done for being so brave, Callie. And thank you, Mrs Peters.'

'That pip's got green bogeys on it,' he heard a high-pitched voice say. 'Yuck!'

Renzo didn't hear the rest of the conversation as he was busy with his own first patient, but he was pretty sure it would involve a special sticker for her patient and a reassuring smile for the mum. Just as he would've done, had he been the doctor treating young Callie.

Professionally, on first impressions he liked Jenna a lot. But he wasn't going to act on the pull of attraction he felt towards her. He'd learned the hard way not to risk his heart again. He'd lost too much, last time. His marriage, his daughter and his belief in love.

'I need both of you for the next case,' Laney said when Jenna and Lorenzo emerged from seeing their last patients. 'Billy Jackson is three. He fell on the stairs an hour ago and cut his forehead.'

Badly enough to need stitches rather than glueing the cut together, Lorenzo assumed, or Laney wouldn't have asked for them both to see the boy.

'Let's go and have a look at you and sort out that cut, Billy,' Lorenzo said with a smile when they went out to see the little boy.

Billy looked anxious and shielded the cut with his hand. 'I don't want to. It hurts.'

'I promise you we'll try our best to stop it hurting,' Lorenzo said, crouching down to the little boy's level. 'Do you like cars?'

Billy nodded solemnly and clutched his mother's hand.

'So do I. Tell you what, while I'm looking at your poorly head, do you want to look through all my pictures of cars and see which one is your favourite?'

Again, Billy nodded.

'That's great. I'm Dr Renzo, and this is Dr Jenna. And I promise we're going to make your head feel much less sore.' He took a pack of cards from his pocket and handed them to Billy, straightened up and looked at the little boy's mum. 'Are you OK, Mrs Jackson?'

She gave him a rueful smile. 'Just about. There was an awful lot of blood. That's why I brought him into the emergency department—and they sent us up to you.'

'Head wounds always bleed a lot, and they always look much more scary than they really are,' Lorenzo said, to reassure her.

'Do you know how Billy banged his head?' Jenna asked.

'He tripped while he was going upstairs and he banged his head on one of the treads,' Mrs Jackson said.

'We see lots of children who've done exactly that,' Jenna said reassuringly. 'Was he unconscious at all after he banged his head, or has he seemed woozy since then or wanted to go to sleep?'

'No. He started crying the moment it happened.'

'Probably from the fright he gave himself, as well as the pain of the cut,' Jenna said. 'But it's good that he wasn't unconscious or woozy—that means he probably doesn't have concussion. I know it must've been a real worry for you but, as Renzo said, it's a lot less serious than it looks. Would you like to sit on the bed with Billy while we take a look at his cut and do a couple of tests?'

Between them, Lorenzo and Jenna took a closer look at the cut—a long gash, though thankfully it didn't have jagged edges—and then they checked his pupils and his reaction to light.

'I'm happy that we're looking at a straightforward cut rather than concussion or anything to worry about,' Lorenzo said. 'It's quite a big cut, so we're going to need to put stitches in. But I promise it's not going to hurt, Billy. I'm going to put some magic cream on your head so you won't feel anything when I mend your cut, and before that I'm going to ask Dr Jenna to help you to breathe in some gas and air. It's a bit like the stuff you get in a balloon when you've been to a party.'

'A balloon?' Billy's eyes went round with amazement. 'Will I go up in the air?'

Jenna clearly heard the slight panic in his voice because she said, 'No, sweetie, I promise you won't. You'll still be sitting there right next to Mummy.'

'And meanwhile you have a job to do,' Lorenzo said, gesturing to the cards Billy was holding. 'Have a look through these cars and tell me which one is your favourite.'

Jenna administered the gas and air, and Lorenzo put anaesthetic gel on the wound.

'Can you feel me touching your head?' Lorenzo asked.

'No-o,' Billy said, sounding surprised.

'That's good. Now, tell me about the cars you like best,' Lorenzo said.

While Billy held his mum's hand very tightly and looked through the car pictures, exclaiming every so often about one he liked, Lorenzo closed the wound with six neat, careful stitches.

'The good news is that the stitches are dissolvable, so you won't have to come and have them taken out again,' Jenna said to Mrs Jackson. 'I'll run you through how to care for the wound and I'll give you a leaflet as well, because obviously right now you're worried sick about Billy and it's hard to concentrate and remember things when you're worried. Basically you need to keep the area dry for the next two days, but you can wash it quickly with soap and water and pat it dry after that. If the wound opens up or looks red and swollen, or there's any kind of discharge, bring him straight back.'

'Thank you. I will,' Mrs Jackson said.

'So which one's your favourite out of the ones you liked, Billy?' Lorenzo asked when he'd finished the last suture.

'This one.' Billy handed him a card with a picture of a red sports car.

'Good choice. That's my favourite, too.'

'Because it's red?' the little boy guessed.

'Because it's Italian, like me,' Lorenzo said with a smile.

Billy's eyes widened. 'Have you got a real car like that?'

Lorenzo chuckled. 'I wish! Maybe one day.'

'I want a car like that when I'm all growed up,' Billy said.

'That sounds like a good plan,' Lorenzo said. He took a glittery sticker from his pocket with the words 'I was THIS brave' emblazoned across it. 'And I'm giving you a special sticker so you can show everyone else how brave you were today.'

'Thank you,' Billy said. With a shy look at his mother first, he handed the rest of the cards back to Lorenzo.

'Thank you,' Lorenzo said. He smiled at Mrs Jackson. 'Try not to worry. I know Jenna's taken you through what to look out for, but if you're concerned at all come back and see us.'

'I will,' she said. 'Thank you so much for what you've done for Billy.'

'Pleasure,' Lorenzo said. 'Take the stairs a bit more slowly from now on, Billy, OK?'

The little boy nodded.

'Nice work,' Jenna said when Billy and his mother had gone. 'So you use car pictures to distract little boys?'

'Not just boys. Girls like cars, too,' Lorenzo said. 'But I have a backup set of cards with puppies and kittens, to distract the kids who don't like cars.'

'Know your patient, hmm?' Jenna asked.

'Something like that.'

She glanced at her watch. 'It's almost lunchtime. Are you already spoken for?'

Lorenzo felt his eyes widen. Was she asking him out? He didn't have a problem with a woman taking the lead and asking a man out—but, considering they'd only just met, this was too fast for his liking. And he wasn't in the market for dating anyway.

'For lunch, that is,' she added swiftly. 'As this is your first day, if you don't already have plans, then you're very welcome to come to the canteen with me if you'd like some company and someone to show you where things are.'

Not a date, then: a colleague simply being kind and offering to show him around his new place of work. He could manage that. 'Thanks. That'd be nice.'

'Don't thank me just yet,' she warned.

'Why?' he asked, confused. 'Is the food not very nice here?'

'It's nothing to do with the food,' she said. 'Actually, I'll buy your lunch as I have a proposition for you.'

Lorenzo was pretty sure that it was just a turn of phrase, but the word 'proposition' put all sorts of inappropriate ideas in his head. Jenna Harris was gorgeous as well as being bubbly, with her mop of blonde curls that she wore pulled back in a scrunchie on the ward, wide blue eyes and ready smile. He liked the way she'd been with their patients and their parents: kind, clear and sympathetic.

But, after what had happened with Georgia and Florence, he wasn't up for falling in love again and getting his heart well and truly trampled on. This was his new start, and he intended to focus on his job, not his personal life.

'Proposition,' he said carefully.

'I'll explain over lunch. Meet you back here after your next patient?' she asked.

'OK,' he said.

At the canteen, Lorenzo chose a sandwich, fruit and coffee, and Jenna did the same.

'You really don't have to buy me lunch,' he said while they queued to pay.

'Oh, but I do,' she corrected, 'because I want you to feel ever so slightly beholden to me.'

So she was being manipulative? That was pretty much how Georgia had been with him. Except Jenna was being up front about it instead of hiding secrets. Well, he'd try to keep an open mind and listen to what she had to say before he made any judgements.

Once they'd sat down, he asked, 'So what's the proposition?'

Her eyes widened. 'Hang on, aren't we supposed to be doing all the usual pleasantries first? Like, where did you train, what made you pick paediatrics, does your family live near, that sort of thing?'

He shrugged. 'OK. I trained in London, I picked paediatrics because it was my favourite rotation when I was training; my parents, brother and sister all live in East London at the moment but my parents are thinking of moving back to their roots in Lake Garda when my father retires; and I'm single.' Most importantly, he added, 'And I'm not looking for a partner.' He'd had completely the wrong idea about his marriage, thinking that he and Georgia were happy. But things hadn't been what they'd seemed; he'd lived a lie for nearly two years before Georgia had finally cracked and told him the truth about Florence. Though he kept that particular black hole behind high walls and barbed wire. 'You?'

'I trained here in Muswell Hill, and I chose paediatrics for the same reason as you—I like kids and I really love making them better. My parents and my sister all live in London, about half an hour away from me; and I'm also single and not looking for a partner.' She smiled. 'Which means that you and I can be friends.'

'Is this part of the proposition?' he checked.

She laughed. 'Absolutely not. But we're a close-knit team on our ward and we do a lot of things together. Team nights out for pizza and ten-pin bowling, cinema, picnics on the beach in summer—that sort of thing. It's kind of like having an extended family. Partners and kids come along to half the stuff and it's lovely.'

A family. The thing he'd once had—and lost. And how he missed it. But he knew he was lucky to have what he had: a large extended Italian family who loved him. Wanting more was just greedy.

He shook himself. Jenna didn't know about his past, and she didn't need to know. Besides, she'd clearly meant to reassure him that he'd picked a really nice place to work. 'Sounds good,' he said, forcing himself to keep his tone light.

She raised her coffee mug at him. 'Welcome to the team. I think you're going to love it here as much as I do.'

He hoped so, too, but he'd reserve judgement until he'd been here a while. 'And the proposition?'

'I'm on the ward's fundraising committee. A week on Saturday, we're holding a six-hour danceathon to raise money for new toys for the ward,' she explained. 'People pay a fixed sum to enter, and they can be sponsored either for a flat fee or for each hour they stay on the dance floor.'

Now he understood what the proposition was. 'You want me to be one of the dancers?'

'If you're not on duty, then yes, please.'

Which would be an easy let-out for him. Except she'd know pretty quickly that he wasn't telling the truth, and he didn't want to start his professional life here with a lie. He'd had enough of lies.

'I'm off duty.'

'Good.' She smiled. 'It should be easy for you. Aren't all Italian men meant to be wonderful dancers?'

'That,' he said, 'is a sweeping generalisation. And I'm afraid I'll have to disappoint you, because I have two left feet.'

'So do half the people who are coming along on the day. It really doesn't matter what you look like or how badly you dance, as long as you raise some money for the toys. It's going to be fun,' she said. 'And you'll get to hear Maybe Baby play.'

'Who are Maybe Baby?' he asked.

'They're pretty much the hospital's house band—they play at a lot of weddings and special occasions,' Jenna explained. 'Half of them are from the Maternity ward—Anton on guitar and Gilly on bass—and from our department there's Keely on vocals and Martin on drums. They're fantastic.'

'They're playing for the whole six hours?'

'Probably for about half of it,' she said. 'Nathan, one of the porters in the Emergency Department, is a DJ when he's not working here, so he's doing the other half of the music for us. We're holding the danceathon in the local high school's sports hall; one of the local pubs is running a bar for us and donating the profits from the night, and a few of the parents of children we've treated heard what we're doing and offered to sort out the food for us. Plus we've sweet-talked a few local businesses into donating raffle prizes, everything from nice toiletries to chocolates to vouchers towards a meal.'

Lorenzo had the strongest feeling that she was downplaying her own role in this. Clearly it was something she'd been deeply involved in, something close to her heart.

'I'm more than happy to sponsor someone,'

he said, 'and maybe take tickets on the door or help run your raffle stall. But I'm afraid it's a no to the dancing.'

'It's a shame I can't talk you into it, because it'll be fun,' she said, 'but I'll take the offer of manning a stall, for however much time you can spare. Thank you.'

'Are you dancing?' he asked, suddenly curious.

'Absolutely. You'd never get me running or struggling to lift stuff in the gym, because that doesn't appeal to me in the slightest,' she said, 'but I do a couple of dance classes a week and I walk my neighbour's dog at weekends. That's my preferred way of keeping fit.'

He should back off. It was none of his business. And he wasn't supposed to start being interested in someone else. This was *work*. But he couldn't stop the question coming out. 'What sort of dance classes?'

'Salsa on Tuesdays and Latin ballroom dancing on Thursdays. I'm not elegant enough to do the waltz or the foxtrot,' she explained, 'but I love dancing the samba and the cha-cha-cha.'

The fun and bouncy stuff. That didn't surprise him. From what he'd seen of her so far, that summed up Jenna Harris very neatly. 'So was the danceathon your idea?'

'Guilty as charged.' She raised an eyebrow. 'But everyone else on the committee said it sounded like a lot of fun, or we wouldn't have done it.'

'OK. Count me in for helping on a stall,' he said. And then his mouth ran away with him. He was supposed to be keeping things professional and slightly distant, not putting himself in a position where he'd see more of her. But the words came out anyway. 'I can help set up, too, if you like.'

'Thank you.' She smiled at him. 'And maybe I can talk you into just one dance.'

'Maybe. No promises,' he warned.

'Sure.' Her smile broadened, which told him she had every intention of breaking down his resistance.

Well, she had no chance there. His intentions were stronger still: to keep a professional distance between himself and Jenna. Yes, she was attractive and he liked her very much—but he wasn't risking his heart again. As far as he was concerned, they were strictly colleagues.

'I guess we ought to get back,' he said. 'Thank you for lunch.'

'My pleasure. And thank you for agreeing to help with the danceathon.'

'Prego,' he said, inclining his head. 'You're welcome.'

'If only you'd joined us a month ago. I bet you could've charmed a ton of money out of everyone who walked through the hospital doors by smiling at them and speaking in Italian. You would've been our secret weapon.' She looked at him with narrowed eyes. 'Would you be good at general knowledge, by any chance?'

'I'm reasonable,' he said.

'You're polite, so I'm guessing you're understating your talents because you don't want to boast about how good you are. Right. That settles it. I'm co-opting you onto our departmental quiz team, too.'

'You,' he said, 'are scary. All that sweet, sweet smile, baby-blue eyes and butter-wouldn't-melt expression—but you've got everyone organised and agreeing to things before they even have time to blink, haven't you?'

'Jenna the hustler—that's me,' she said,

looking totally unrepentant. 'If I could actually play pool, I'd make gazillions out of unwary punters and we'd have the best-equipped paediatric department in the country.'

He couldn't help laughing. Even though he wanted to keep her at a distance, her warmth, her charm and her sheer chutzpah were irresistible. He would've liked to find something about her that wiped out that pull of attraction. But even her bossiness had a charm to it. She was *nice*. He'd have to rely on the determination that had got him through the miserable months when his marriage imploded, and keep things professional between them. 'I have a feeling you're going to get a ton of money out of your danceathon. And I bet you'll drive a hard bargain with a toy shop afterwards.'

'Cost price, that's what I'm after,' she said. 'So if you know someone with contacts to a wholesaler or a toy shop, I'm all ears.'

'Sorry. I can't help with that one.'

'That's OK. You're helping me set up, you're manning a stall for a bit, and you agreed to one dance. That'll do nicely.'

Lorenzo was pretty sure he hadn't actually agreed to one dance. But he was equally sure that Jenna wasn't going to let him get away with it. 'Let's get back to the ward,' he said. Where he'd be able to focus on work, and have the space to damp down the unexpected feelings that were threatening to turn him upside down.

CHAPTER TWO

'OH, NOW, THAT smells fabulous,' Jenna said, walking into the kitchen and hugging her twin. 'Tell me that's your lasagne cooking in the oven, Lu.'

'It is.' Lucy hugged her back. 'It'll be ready in twenty minutes. Grab a glass of wine. Will's in the living room with his nose in a book. How was your day?'

'Fine.' Jenna poured herself half a glass of wine. 'The new senior reg started today.'

'What's he or she like?'

'He's nice. Robert asked me to look after him in the PAU today.'

Lucy smiled. 'Because you, my dear sister, are brilliant at tucking new people under your wing.'

'Because I had a good example to follow in the best primary school teacher ever,' Jenna pointed out, and lifted her glass in a toast. 'So how was your day?'

'Fine. Ava spent the whole day chatting.'

Jenna grinned. 'That's because she takes after her aunt.'

'Strictly speaking—' Lucy began.

'I'm her *aunt*,' Jenna said firmly. 'Lu, we've been through this enough times. In every way, Ava is your and Will's daughter. All I did was lend you my womb for a few months—which I know you would have done for me if our situations had been the other way round.'

'Of course I would.' Lucy bit her lip. 'Though the egg was yours, too.'

'And, as we're identical twins, that means our genes are the same, so my egg is exactly the same as yours would've been,' Jenna reminded her. 'As far as I'm concerned, Ava's biologically yours, as well as legally and morally.'

Their friends and family—apart from one notable exception—had all been supportive about the surrogate pregnancy, but Jenna knew Lucy felt guilty about it. And usually Lucy's doubts came to the surface when someone had upset her on the subject.

'Has someone said something to you?' she asked gently.

'No—well, yes,' Lucy admitted.

'I hope you told them to walk a mile in your shoes and learn a few facts before they give you any more of their uninformed opinions.'

Lucy winced. 'It's my fault. The subject of surrogacy came up at toddler group. I should've just kept my mouth shut.'

'You have nothing to be ashamed of. If anything, your story might actually help someone who's struggling with the same issues you went through, and could see that there might just be a light for them, too, at the end of the tunnel.' Jenna sighed. 'But we seem to live in an age where everyone thinks their opinion is more valid than anyone else's, and they don't consider anyone else's feelings before they open their mouths.' Someone had clearly hectored her sister on the subject of surrogate babies. Jenna would've quite liked a serious chat with whoever had been so thoughtless, so she could put them very straight on the subject—and then shake them very hard until their teeth rattled.

'I guess.'

Jenna frowned. 'Lu, you know Ava's *yours*.' Had Lucy not been in a serious car crash which had ruptured her womb and damaged both her ovaries, five years ago, she wouldn't have needed an emergency hysterectomy at the age of twenty-seven, putting an end to any hope of having her own children naturally.

'I know.'

Jenna's frown deepened. 'Please tell me whoever it was didn't say something as vile as Danny did.'

'No-o.'

Which meant they had and Lucy didn't want to admit it. Jenna put her glass on the worktop and hugged her twin. 'Listen to me, you numpty. I love Will dearly, but purely as a brother. I don't fancy him and I never have. He doesn't fancy me, either. He'd drive me absolutely crackers if I had to live with him and all his vague professor stuff—just as I'd drive him crackers by bossing him around and organising him down to the last second instead of letting him get away with it, the way you do. And I love you more than anyone else in the world, Lu. I offered to be your surrogate because I was the one person who could actually make things right again after the adoption agency turned you and Will down. I hated seeing you with a broken heart and I desperately wanted to be able to help you. Just as you would've done, if it had been me in your shoes. And you already know all that, Lu, so I don't know why I need to tell you again.'

Lucy swallowed hard. 'I know.'

'So please don't listen to some over-opinionated, thoughtless woman who clearly doesn't have a clue what it's like to be in that situation or care how she makes other people feel.'

Lucy swallowed hard. 'But I do feel guilty, Jen. If it wasn't for me, you'd be married to Danny by now.'

'And we'd probably be divorced,' Jenna pointed out dryly. 'Marrying him would've been a huge mistake.'

Lucy frowned. 'Would it? Because I worry that you're lonely.'

'I don't need a partner to have a fulfilling life,' Jenna said firmly. She wasn't going to admit to her twin in a million years that yes, sometimes she did feel lonely, when she woke at three in the morning and couldn't sleep. 'And I definitely don't need a partner who's going to issue ultimatums every time I suggest something that doesn't fit in with his world view. Any man who asks me to choose between him and you is going to lose—every single time.' She sang a snatch from the old song 'Sisters', just to emphasise the point, and hugged Lucy again. 'Danny lacked compassion. If anything, you did me a favour, because his reaction to the surrogacy is what made me finally realise that he saw everything in terms of financial cost.'

'But being our surrogate lost you your relationship.'

'Which wouldn't have worked in the long run, believe me. I don't want to be with someone who puts a price on everything and can't see any value if it can't be counted in cash. That isn't how I see things, and that kind of attitude makes me really unhappy. Marrying Danny would've been a disaster.'

'With the IVF treatment and the pregnancy, it cost you a year out of your career,' Lucy persisted.

'Which I can make up.'

'And it hit your earnings.'

That had been one of Danny's biggest arguments, and Jenna had despised him for it.

Some things were way, way more important than money. Like her sister's happiness. Family. *Love.* 'I really don't care about the money, Lu. I had savings, and you and Will helped out with my rent. We managed just fine. It isn't an issue.'

'You've got an answer for everything, haven't you?' Lucy asked with a sigh.

'Yup. So, oh, best sister in the world, try to stop worrying about it and let me go and take a peek at my gorgeous niece—and I promise not to wake her.'

'I love you,' Lucy said.

'I love you, too,' Jenna said with a smile.

She tiptoed upstairs and crept into the nursery; Ava was fast asleep in her cot, with her hands thrown back over her head, looking totally angelic. Although Jenna had given birth to the baby, she'd always considered Ava as being Lucy's, not hers. And the love she felt for Ava wasn't that of a mother: it was that of a doting aunt. Which was just how it should be, in her view.

'Sleep tight, my beautiful niece,' she whispered, and tiptoed out of the nursery.

Back down in the kitchen, Will had joined Lucy and greeted Jenna with a hug.

'Perfect timing,' Lucy said with a smile, and served up.

Jenna took one mouthful and sighed in bliss. 'You really do make the best lasagne in the world.'

'And at least I know you're going to eat properly when you have dinner with us on Monday nights,' Lucy said.

'I *do* eat properly,' Jenna protested.

'Not when you're really busy on the ward, you don't. You grab a chocolate bar or a bowl of cereal.'

Jenna grinned. 'You do exactly the same when you're up to your eyes in baseline assessments in the first three weeks of the new school year and Will's forgotten the time and that it was his turn to cook that night.'

'I don't forget the time,' Will protested.

The sisters looked at him and laughed. 'Oh, you do, honey,' Lucy said, and leaned over to kiss him. 'Half the time you live in the first century, not the twenty-first.'

'It's my job,' Will said. 'And I'll join Lu in nagging you about eating properly, too, Jen.'

'Oh, give me a break!' But Jenna was laughing, knowing that her brother-in-law meant well. 'Now the new senior reg has started, it should be a bit less frantic on the ward.'

'So what's the new doctor like?' Will asked.

'He's good with kids. He has two packs of cards in his pockets as distractions—one with cars and one with puppies. It came in handy today when we had a toddler who slipped on the stairs and banged his head badly enough to need stitches,' Jenna said.

'Cars,' Will said dryly, 'shouldn't be gender specific.'

'Agreed, and Renzo isn't sexist. He says that girls also like cars.' Jenna smiled. 'But that might be because he's Italian and he loves fast cars and thinks everyone else does, too. He and little Billy—the lad who needed stitches—were practically drooling over this sports car.'

'I'd be drooling over that, too. Except we wouldn't be able to fit a baby seat in it,' Will said.

'Italian,' Lucy said thoughtfully.

'No, no and no,' Jenna said, knowing exactly what was going through her twin's mind. *Tall, dark and gorgeous.* Which pretty much summed up Lorenzo Conti. She definitely wasn't going to tell Lucy that he was single, because she knew her sister would go straight into matchmaker mode. 'But he did agree to help at the danceathon.'

'That's good. Though I still feel guilty about not being able to make it,' Lucy said.

'You have Will's niece's wedding in Edinburgh. And Will's parents need some catch-up time with Ava,' Jenna reminded her. 'You both gave me a massive donation and a raffle prize, so you've more than done your bit.'

'We wanted to help,' Will said.

'And you have. A lot,' Jenna said. 'So how's your day been, Will?'

'Full of deciphering illegible student hand-writing—I swear it's twice as bad on exam papers,' Will said with a groan.

'Ah, the joys of May,' Jenna teased, laughing; she knew how much her brother-in-law loved his job and he adored his students—just as they adored him.

It was the perfect family evening, and Jenna was thoroughly relaxed by the time she got home. Though she couldn't quite get Lorenzo Conti out of her head. He'd been very adamant about being single and not looking for a partner; it sounded to her as if someone had really hurt him. Or maybe he'd lost someone to illness or an accident and didn't want to risk his heart again because the loss had hurt him too much. Not that it was any of her business. And she absolutely wasn't interested in anything other than a professional relationship with her new colleague. After Danny, as far as she was concerned, love was completely off limits. She didn't trust her judgement any more, not after she'd got it so badly wrong with him. She had a family she adored and a job that fulfilled her. She was lucky. Wanting to have the same kind of closeness with someone that Lucy had with Will, and a baby of her own—that would just be greedy.

Jenna's first patient in clinic the next morning, eight-year-old Maddie Loveday, was a puzzle.

'It started six weeks ago,' Maddie's mum said. 'She'd been at football club and came home with really red cheeks. It looked a bit like windburn, but it seemed a bit odd because it's not that cold and windy at the end of April. Then she went down with a really nasty virus. It hit the whole family and even I was in bed for three days with it.'

A rash and a virus. Two things that were really hard to narrow down, and half the time there wasn't an effective treatment and you just had to wait it out. Jenna smiled and waited for Mrs Loveday to continue.

'The rash didn't go away and it spread down her arms and legs. She said her legs hurt, she had pains in her tummy, and it hurt to swallow.' Mrs Loveday grimaced. 'Then she was really down and a bit weepy—which just isn't my Maddie. I took her to the doctor.'

'What did your GP say?' Jenna asked.

'He thought it might be allergic eczema, but my youngest has eczema and I'm really careful with laundry detergent and conditioner. Maddie's never had any kind of reaction to food, and that rash didn't look like any eczema I've ever seen.' Mrs Loveday sighed. 'I think he referred Maddie here just to shut me up.'

Seeing that she was close to tears, Jenna put a reassuring hand on her arm. 'Mrs Loveday, when our mums tell us that their kids aren't right, we listen. You're the experts on your kids, so you know when there's something wrong. It's our job to listen and help you.'

'Thank you.' Mrs Loveday swallowed hard. 'I know you can't believe everything you read on the Internet, but I wondered if the rash was some kind of autoimmune thing.'

'That's a possibility,' Jenna said. 'Rashes have lots of different causes and they can be really tricky to diagnose. And you're absolutely right not to believe everything you read on the Internet, because there are a lot of scaremongering stories out there.' She turned to the little girl. 'Maddie, is it OK if I examine you?'

Maddie nodded.

Jenna looked at the rash. Coupled with the pain in Maddie's legs and tummy, and her difficulty in swallowing, the rash could well be a sign of an autoimmune problem, but Jenna wasn't sure quite which one. 'I've not seen a rash like this before,' she said. 'I think you're right, Mrs Loveday, and it's very likely an autoimmune disease. Do you mind if I have a quick discussion with one of my more senior colleagues?'

'As long as you can find out what's wrong with Maddie and make her better, then do whatever you need to,' Mrs Loveday said.

Jenna headed for the offices. None of the consultants was around, but Lorenzo was in his office. Given that he was her senior and had three or four years' more experience than she did, there was a chance that he'd seen a condition like Maddie's before. She rapped on his office door. 'Renzo, have you got a minute, please?'

'Sure,' he said.

'How are you on autoimmune diseases?'

'I've treated a few in my time,' he said. 'What are you looking at?'

'I'm not entirely sure.' She filled him in on Maddie Loveday's medical history and symptoms. 'I can see you're busy, so I'm sorry to ask, but I'm a bit stuck. I don't suppose I could borrow you to come and have a look at her, could I?'

'Sure,' he said, to her relief, and saved the file he was working on.

After Jenna had introduced him to the Lovedays, Lorenzo examined Maddie's skin. 'Mrs Loveday, has anyone talked to you about juvenile dermatomyositis or JDM?' he asked.

Mrs Loveday looked surprised. 'No. The GP just sent me here.'

'It's pretty rare, with about three in a million children being affected, and girls are twice as likely as boys to have it,' Lorenzo said. 'Basically "dermatomyositis" means inflammation of the skin and muscles, and from what Jenna's already told me and what I can see here, it looks to me as if that's what's happening to Maddie.'

'What causes it?' Mrs Loveday asked.

'We don't actually know,' Lorenzo said. 'Jenna told me about Maddie's virus, and in the cases we know of there was a virus involved.'

'So how long does it last? Will it ever go away? Is she going to get worse?' Mrs Loveday asked.

'Sometimes a child has one episode of JDM that lasts for a couple of years and then goes away for ever; sometimes it comes back again after a few years of remission; and sometimes it doesn't go away at all and needs managing for the rest of the child's life,' Lorenzo said. 'I'm sorry to be so vague, but the way the condition develops really varies. What I can promise is that we'll sort out some treatment so Maddie can live her life just as if she hasn't got JDM.'

'So what does this JDM do?' Mrs Loveday asked.

'It makes the muscles weaker and causes pain, so that's why Maddie's talked about her legs hurting and having tummy pains,' Lorenzo said. 'The inflammation tends to affect the large muscles around the hips and shoulders, so that means it's harder for Maddie to walk, climb the stairs, get up from the floor or lift her arms. And it'll make you tired, Maddie.'

The little girl nodded. 'Since I got the rash and tummy pains, I can't run as fast when I play football, and I'm really tired by the end of the match.'

'So how do you treat it?' Mrs Loveday asked.

'Medication and physiotherapy. I'd like to admit her to the ward for now,' Lorenzo said. 'Maddie might need to stay for a couple of weeks so we can get her condition under control—we can give her some medication to help, but there will be other treatments as well. We'll start with steroids at first and that'll really help with her muscles and her skin.'

Mrs Loveday looked shocked. 'Steroids? Isn't that the stuff bodybuilders use?'

'No, these are corticosteroids,' Jenna explained. 'They're naturally produced by the body, too, and we use them to bring down inflammation—that will stop Maddie's muscles hurting and it will also sort out the rash.'

'We'll also need to do some tests, including an EMG,' Lorenzo said. 'That's a special scan which shows us the electrical activities in your muscles—and I promise it doesn't hurt, Maddie.'

'Good,' the little girl said. 'Because I really, really hurt right now and I hate feeling like this every day. I just want to play football.'

'We'll make it stop hurting,' Jenna promised.

'We have physiotherapists here who can teach you some exercises, Maddie, to make your muscles work better,' Lorenzo said.

'They'll make you work hard,' Jenna added, 'but they'll make it fun. You can come along, too, Mrs Loveday, and learn how to do the exercises at home with Maddie.'

'Will they be like the exercises I do at football?' Maddie asked.

'Possibly,' Jenna said.

'Because I don't want to stop playing football. I want to be a footballer when I grow up and be captain of the women's team for England. I won't have to stop playing, will I?' she asked, looking miserable at the thought of giving up the sport she clearly loved more than anything else.

'Definitely not,' Lorenzo said. 'And I know it's horrible feeling so ill, but I reckon you timed getting ill just right—the football season's over, so it means you won't miss out on matches over the summer.'

'But there's football training camp in August. Will I be better for that?' Maddie asked.

'Right now, we don't know how you're going to respond to the treatment and if we'll need to change your medication, but we'll do our best to make you well enough for the camp,' Jenna said.

'Once we've got the rash and the pain under control with the steroids,' Lorenzo said, 'you might need some other medication, Maddie. We'll see how things go, but you might need to have methotrexate injections once a week—the nurse should be able to do that at your family doctor's surgery, so you won't have to come back to hospital for it—and an anti-sickness medication.'

'Steroids sometimes affect your bone density—that means how strong your bones are—so we'll also need to give you special calcium and vitamin D supplements,' Jenna said.

'And, once you're responding to the treatment, we'll decrease the steroids gradually,' Lorenzo explained. 'If you do have a flare-up in the future, then we'll know which drugs work best for you and we can make sure you get the right ones to treat any future episodes.'

'You'll need to make sure you use plenty of sun cream and wear a hat in the summer,' Jenna added.

'Coach always makes us put sun cream on before training,' Maddie said.

'That's good. So we'll admit you to the ward now,' Lorenzo said, 'and try and get you all ready for football camp. Once you're home, we'll see you every few months to see how you're getting on and if we need to change your medication at all.'

Once Jenna had got one of the nurses to settle Maddie on the ward, she arranged the tests that Lorenzo had recommended. The EMG confirmed Lorenzo's diagnosis; and she noticed that he gave up his lunch break to sit and chat to the little girl about football.

Lorenzo Conti was definitely one of the good guys.

She liked the way he worked, reassuring both their patients and their parents; and with him she really felt part of a team. It felt as if she'd worked with him for years, rather than only a couple of days. Which was crazy. She couldn't have that kind of rapport with him so soon.

In their afternoon break, she caught him just as he was heading for the staff room. 'I owe you cake for helping me with Maddie,' she said.

'You really don't. I was just doing my job, the same as you,' he said with a smile.

'You taught me something new today and I appreciate that, plus I happen to know you didn't have a lunch break—you spent it talking to Maddie about football,' she pointed out.

He shrugged. 'Maddie was fretting and I wanted to help her settle in to the ward. We had a fabulous argument about whether Italian football players were better than English ones, and that really cheered her up.'

Jenna could just imagine. Lorenzo had worked out the best way to take the little girl's mind off her illness and played his part with gusto. He was the kind of colleague it was a joy to work with. 'I just want to say thank you—I didn't want you to think I'm taking you for granted,' she said.

There was an odd expression on his face, but for so briefly that she thought she might have imagined it.

'I know you're not taking me for granted. We're colleagues. I'm just doing my job,' Lorenzo said. 'You really don't need to buy me cake.'

Then a really nasty thought hit her. Did he think that she was coming on to him? But she wasn't. 'I'd make the same offer to any of my colleagues who helped me like that,' she said. 'Regardless of gender or age.' And she hoped he'd follow through with the rest: regardless of marital status, because it was a platonic offer rather than a come-on.

'It's fine,' he said.

'Well, thanks. I really did appreciate your help,' she said. 'I thought Maddie might have some kind of rheumatology issue, but I haven't come across JDM before.'

'To be fair, I've only seen one case, and I wasn't the lead doctor in the case,' Lorenzo said.

'I'll look it up in my books tonight after salsa class.' She smiled. 'Which is a double-win situation for me, because it means I can find out what I need to know for Maddie's treatment, and revise for my paediatrics exams.'

Lorenzo stared at her. 'You're, what, three or four years younger than me?'

'I'm thirty-two.'

'Three years, then. I'm surprised you're not through all your exams already.'

'That's because I took a year's sabbatical,' she said.

'Sabbatical?'

His voice was soft and gentle, and Jenna almost confided in him about why she'd taken time off work. Then Danny's voice echoed in her head: *'You're going to be a surrogate mum for your sister? That's the most stupid idea I've ever heard. What about your career? How can you throw all that away just for a kid that you're not even keeping?'*

She didn't think Lorenzo was anything like Danny, but the situation wasn't exactly the easiest to explain. She didn't want him thinking that either she was a saint—because she was far from that—or the naive idiot Danny had called her when she'd refused to give in to his haranguing. 'Life throws up unexpected stuff, sometimes,' she said with a smile, fudging the issue.

* * *

Lorenzo had seen Jenna work with their patients. He knew she was competent, and also she was confident enough to admit when something was outside her experience, as Maddie had been today—so he didn't think she'd taken a year off because she'd been struggling with her work and needed to think about her future. So why had she taken a year's sabbatical? Had it been a career break to have a baby, perhaps?

Though, in his experience, when his colleagues had children, they tended to talk about them. Jenna hadn't said a word about having children of her own.

Maybe she'd had a child, then lost it.

He knew how that felt, and he didn't talk about it. He could understand why someone just wouldn't want the constant reminders of the empty spaces in their lives. So he wasn't going to push her about it. Besides, she'd hit the nail on the head about his own situation. Unexpected stuff. In his case, it had been something he'd been too naive and stupid to work out for himself. That his wife had cheated on him with her ex, and the little girl he'd believed was his was actually another man's daughter. 'Very true,' he said. 'Life can be unexpected.' And sometimes it took you a while to pick yourself up and dust yourself off again. 'If you want anyone to test you on stuff before the exams, give me a yell.'

'Thanks. That's kind.' She smiled at him, and he had to damp down the urge to lace his fingers through hers and suggest something more personal than simply exam revision.

This was ridiculous. They'd both said that they weren't in the market for a relationship. After Georgia, he'd lost his capacity to trust.

Yet something about Jenna Harris drew him. Her warmth, her verve, her kindness.

He was going to have to be careful about this. Really careful.

Because he really didn't want to risk his heart again.

CHAPTER THREE

By the end of Lorenzo's first two weeks at Muswell Hill Memorial, he'd completely settled in to his new role. As Jenna had told him on the first day, the team on the ward was good to work with, and they were like a family. He'd already been to a team pizza night out, a weekend game of football in the park, and joined the ward's quiz team—and the danceathon was happening at the weekend. It felt as if he'd been working at Muswell Hill for months rather than a matter of a few days.

The only thing he needed to deal with now was his inappropriate feelings towards Jenna.

Every time his hand brushed against hers at work, he felt a tingle all the way down his arm. When she smiled, it made his heart feel as if it had just skipped a beat. And this was crazy. He didn't want to get involved and he knew that she didn't, either.

He really didn't understand why he was reacting to her in this way. It would be easier if she'd turned out to be a gossip, or an ambition-driven bitch who trampled on her colleagues to get a promotion—the kind of person he wouldn't want to be within a mile of. But she was warm, sweet, great with their patients and parents, and he'd seen her patiently explaining something to one of the junior doctors.

And he had to admit he was attracted to her. Physically as well as intellectually. The problem was, he'd been here before with Georgia. He'd fallen in love with someone he thought loved him back— and she'd let him down in the worst possible way. He'd pretty much come to terms with the fact that Georgia had left him for someone else; although it had hurt, he could understand that if you loved someone that much it just took you over and you couldn't help your feelings. But taking their daughter away had hurt him more deeply than anything he'd ever known. He had no intention of risking that sort of pain again.

Besides, for someone as nice as Jenna to be

single and adamant that she wasn't looking for a relationship, he'd guess that she'd been let down by someone in the past. Something to do with her year off work, perhaps. Not that he could be intrusive and ask.

So he'd have to keep his feelings under control. Remind himself that relationships weren't for him, and he was Jenna's colleague. Maybe they could become friends—but he wasn't sure he could even handle that.

Strictly professional was the order of the day.

On Saturday afternoon, Lorenzo walked to the local high school and signed in, then followed the signs to the sports hall. Jenna was already there. He noticed that her hair was caught back in a scrunchie, the way it was at work, and he wondered what it would be like if she took the scrunchie out. Would her hair fall over her shoulders in wild curls?

Worst of all, he found himself wondering what her hair would look like spread over his pillow...

Oh, for pity's sake. This was a charity danceathon. This wasn't the time or the place to start fantasising about Jenna Harris. She was off limits and they had work to do. He shook himself mentally, then went over to her. 'Reporting for duty, as promised,' he said with a smile. 'What do you need me to do?'

Jenna looked up at Lorenzo and her heart skipped a beat. Instead of the formal shirt, tie and dark trousers he always wore on the ward beneath his white coat, he was wearing jeans and a T-shirt. It made him look younger and more approachable; and she was horrified to find that she was actually reaching out to put her hand on his arm.

Absolutely not.

This wasn't the deal. He was helping out. He was here as a new colleague and nothing more. She needed to keep this strictly professional.

She shook herself. 'Hi. Thanks for coming to help.' He'd asked her what she wanted him to do. Her head was suddenly full of all sorts of inappropriate phrases. She managed to get a grip on herself—just—and said, 'There's a table over there with all the raffle prizes on it. If you wouldn't mind taping raffle ticket numbers to the prizes, and then folding the rest of the raffle tickets for the box, that would be great.' She handed him a book

of raffle tickets and a roll of sticky tape; her
fingers brushed against his and a shiver ran
down her spine.

Was it her imagination, or had his eyes just
widened slightly?

Or was she reading too much into it?

This really wasn't the time or the place.

Tickets, she reminded herself sharply.
'We're just using the ones on the right-hand
side of the ticket page that end in a zero to
stick on the prizes, but all the left-hand tickets go in the box, folded so you can't see the
number.'

'Which means there's a one in ten chance
of winning a prize. That sounds reasonable,'
he said, and went off to sort out the raffle
table.

Nathan from the Emergency Department
was helping the members of Maybe Baby to
set up the stage and wire up the sound system
ready for the sound check; the local pub was
setting up the bar to one side of the hall; and
a stream of parents of their former patients
came over to her to check where she wanted
the food set out.

All the time, Jenna was incredibly aware
of Lorenzo's presence. This was crazy. The

last thing she needed in her life right now was any kind of complication. She was busy at work and with her studies, and she liked her life just as it was.

Yet a little voice kept echoing in her head. *What if...?*

What if she could have what Lucy had? Someone who loved her and a family of her own?

She shoved the thought away. Apart from anything else, she had the strongest feeling that Lorenzo had been hurt in the past— hence his insistence on not wanting a relationship. And, given the way her judgement had let her down so badly over Danny, how could she be sure that she wouldn't be making just as much of a mistake with Lorenzo?

She was just going to have to ignore that little voice and listen to her common sense instead.

Once Lorenzo had sorted out the raffle tickets, he joined another team in setting out chairs for the people who'd just come to watch the dancing or who needed a break from the dance floor.

'It's really good of you to do this,' Jenna

said, coming over to him. 'I feel a bit guilty, roping you in to help when you've been working at the hospital for barely a couple of weeks.'

'It's fine. I wasn't doing anything special at the weekend anyway—plus it's a nice way to get to know the team outside work,' he pointed out.

'It's still appreciated,' she said.

He had to muster every gram of professionalism when she smiled at him. What on earth was the matter with him? It was anatomically impossible for your heart to do a somersault, so feeling that it had just happened was utterly ridiculous. He needed to get a grip.

'Is there anything else you need me to do?' he asked.

She shook her head. 'I'm just handing out the cash floats to the hospital-run stalls, and then I'm going to change into my dancing shoes.'

'Then I'll do my best to sell raffle tickets,' Lorenzo said.

When the danceathon started, Lorenzo was surprised to discover just how good the band was. Keely, one of the senior nurses in their department, had a beautiful voice and could easily have made a career out of singing. Nathan, one of the porters in the Emergency Department, was the DJ who did an hour's slot between each set the band played; and, in between sorting out the music, the band and the DJ all joined in with the dancing.

'You've done more than your fair share on the raffle, Renzo. I'll take over while you take a break. Go and have a dance,' Laney, one of the nurses on their ward, said with a smile, taking the box of tickets and the cash box from him.

It looked as if he didn't have much choice, even though dancing really wasn't his thing. He stood on the edge of the dance floor, moving awkwardly to the music and wondering how long he'd have to be there before he could justifiably go back to the raffle table, and then Jenna was there beside him.

'Hey. You've finally come to join us on the dance floor?' she asked.

'Laney bullied me into it. I did warn you that not all Italian men could dance and I have two left feet,' he said with a rueful smile.

'Everyone can dance. You just need someone to show you how,' she said with a grin. 'This is salsa, and it's fun.'

No, it wasn't. He felt like a fish out of water. 'Can't I just move my feet any old how?' he asked plaintively.

She smiled. 'Not to salsa, but I promise the steps aren't so bad. Stand opposite me, and I'll show you. I'll slow it down for you so we do it at half the speed until you get the hang of it. This is the first step they teach you in class—the side basic.'

He stood opposite her, knowing he was just about to make a colossal idiot of himself.

'Now, you're going to mirror everything I do,' she said.

Mirror everything.

He noticed that she'd changed more than just her shoes, as she'd suggested earlier: the faded jeans and ancient T-shirt she'd worn while setting things up had been replaced by black trousers and a strappy top. And her shoes were clearly proper dance shoes, red and glittery. Somehow he wasn't surprised that Jenna had chosen such a bright, sparkly colour. They went perfectly with her personality.

'Stand with your left leg bent, and keep your right leg straight,' she instructed. 'Shift your weight to your right leg.'

Just the same as she was when she gave instructions at work, he noticed: clear, concise and making things easy to follow.

He really liked that about her; yet, at the same time, he was wary. He didn't think she was the sort to hurt other people; but then again he'd believed that about Georgia, and how wrong he'd been there. He'd kept all his relationships strictly platonic, ever since, to make sure he wouldn't get hurt again. But Jenna tempted him more than anyone he'd ever met. Her warmth, her sweetness...

Yet he was pretty sure that she, too, had been hurt in the past. The way she'd avoided talking about her sabbatical was a big clue.

Maybe they could help each other.

Or maybe they'd just make things worse and he should just leave it.

He shook himself, realising that she'd spoken to him. 'Sorry. I missed that. Would you mind running through it again?'

'Sure. Take a step to the left with your left leg,' she said, 'rock back so your weight's on your right leg again, and close your feet. The beat's one, two, three-and-hold.'

Mirroring what she did, he managed to do it without tripping over.

'Now repeat it the other way,' she said. Again, she talked him through it and slowed it down so he could follow.

'Brilliant. Now we put them both together—in dancing everything's a count of eight. So it's one, two, three, hold, five, six, seven, hold.'

He couldn't quite follow her arm movements, but he managed the feet, and she seemed pleased.

'Perfect,' she said. 'We'll make a dancer of you yet. There's a back-and-forward one as well.'

Which sounded a bit too much for his confidence level. 'Let's just leave it at the side one,' he said.

'No problem. We'll stick to the side basic,' she said with a smile. 'Ready?'

He counted the beats. One, two, three, hold... And then somehow he was dancing with her. Really dancing, not just moving randomly and hoping he didn't look too much of an idiot on the dance floor. She was right: it *was* fun. He couldn't remember the last time he'd enjoyed himself so much.

Jenna had taken the scrunchie out of her hair, too, so her curls were free and wild; she was laughing and her blue eyes were sparkling, and she looked utterly beautiful—like a Pre-Raphaelite goddess. He hadn't felt this kind of pull towards someone since he'd first started dating Georgia.

The thought was enough to haul him up short and he missed the beat, stumbled and stopped.

'Are you OK?' Jenna asked.

'Sure.' He smiled at her, not wanting to tell her what was really wrong. 'I've just got two left feet, that's all.'

She smiled back. 'A couple of the guys at our salsa class just couldn't work out which feet to move, so our teacher got them to wear a band on each wrist—lemon for left and red for right—to give them a visual cue, and it really helped.' She shrugged. 'Though I guess this isn't really the place for it.'

She slowed her movements down and talked him through the steps until he was moving confidently again. Jenna was just the same outside work as she was on the ward, kind and considerate without making a big deal of things; Lorenzo really liked that about her.

He danced with her to the rest of the song,

then said, 'It's time for me to go and sell raffle tickets among the crowd.'

Her glance said very clearly that she knew he was chickening out of the dancing; he wondered if she realised why, and that it was her nearness rather than the actual dancing that spooked him.

Did she feel the same pull towards him that he felt towards her? And, if so, what were they going to do about it? Could he take a risk with her?

Even though Lorenzo was officially walking round the seated audience, sweet-talking them into buying more raffle tickets, he still couldn't take his eyes off Jenna. She was dancing a much faster and more complicated salsa with three or four people he guessed might be from her class, because they were keeping up with her and doing all the dipping and swaying and turns—things he was very glad she hadn't suggested that he tried doing, because they were way above his pay grade.

The way she moved was stunning, all sinuous and sensual. He wanted to walk over there, dance with her and then kiss her until they were both dizzy. Which would be a really stupid thing to do. He worked with

Jenna, and they'd agreed to be colleagues and friends. Anything else would just lead to heartache.

He concentrated on selling the raffle tickets until all the prizes had been won, then took Jenna a glass of water.

'Thanks, that's so kind of you.' She drank all the water in one go, and then smiled at him.

And how crazy was it that his heart felt as if it had just done a backward somersault?

He managed to pull himself together. Just. 'All the prizes have been won, so Laney and I are going to count up the money; and she said we need to take off the float.'

'The float was ten pounds. Thank you. There's a box under the table with bags for the coins and rubber bands for the notes, plus a big padded bag to put the whole lot in,' she said.

Clearly Jenna had done this sort of thing before, he thought, because she was perfectly organised.

As if his thoughts had shown on his face, she added, 'With my sister being a teacher, I've helped out at a lot of school events in my time and counted up a lot of takings, so I know the most efficient way to deal with the money afterwards.'

'Got you,' he said.

Between them, he and Laney totted up the takings and wrote them on the outside of the padded bag. And, when Maybe Baby had played the last song of the danceathon, Keely called Jenna on to the stage to round up the evening.

'Thank you, everyone, for coming tonight,' Jenna said. 'And I'd like to thank everyone who's helped at a stall, donated a prize, sponsored a dancer, danced here on the floor tonight or come along for support and bought things. Thank you to all the parents and local businesses who've helped us with food and drink and prizes. We'll total everything up over the weekend and I'll make sure how much we've raised is posted on the ward's website and social media page. And thank you, too, on behalf of our patients, because the toys your money's going to buy will help them settle on the ward and distract them from some of their worries. That really makes a difference and it means that treatment is less stressful for them. Thank you—all of you.'

There was a round of applause, and then the clearing away started. Everyone worked together, moving tables, chairs and the few bits of unsold stock. The band and the DJ cleared away the sound systems and their equipment, and then Jenna wielded a mop and bucket to make sure that the school's sports hall was left spotless.

'Thanks, everyone,' she said when it was all done. 'I've really appreciated your help tonight.'

'Can I give you a hand taking that home?' Lorenzo asked, gesturing to the box that contained all the proceeds from the night.

'I'm definitely not walking about with all this money. I've booked a taxi,' she said. 'You're very welcome to a lift, if you're on my way home.'

This was his get-out, Lorenzo thought. Even if they were going in the same direction, he could say no.

'Actually, come along anyway. I owe you a drink for giving up most of your day and all of your evening,' she added.

'It was my pleasure. You don't owe me anything,' he said. But then his mouth seemed to be working to a different script to the one in his head, and he heard himself saying, 'Though I'll wait with you until the taxi arrives. I know you're perfectly capable of looking after yourself, but you've got tonight's takings with you.'

'And you're right—I'd rather not be on my own with that sort of money,' she said. 'Thank you.'

It was only a few minutes' wait; and then somehow he found himself seeing Jenna home in the taxi anyway.

'Come in for a glass of wine,' she said.

And his mouth was really on a roll, because instead of making a polite excuse he found himself agreeing.

She ushered him into the kitchen and put the box from the danceathon on one of the worktops. 'What would you prefer—red or white?'

'Whatever's open,' he said.

She peered into the fridge. 'Rosé.' She paused. 'Is that OK?'

'It's fine,' he said.

She poured two glasses and handed him one before lifting her own in a toast. 'Cheers, and thank you again for your help.'

'My pleasure.' He took a sip of the wine.

Clearly he'd made a face, because she asked, 'It's too sweet for you, isn't it?'

'It's fine,' he fibbed.

'You said most of your family lives in Italy.' She bit her lip. 'Please don't tell me they have a vineyard.'

'I'm afraid they do,' he said.

'And they've won awards for their wine?' she guessed.

He nodded. 'Bardolino *chiaretto.*'

'That's red, right?'

'Red's the most famous Bardolino wine. But *chiaretto* is rosé,' he said. Light, not too sweet, and perfect for summer evenings.

'Sorry, I'm afraid this isn't award-winning stuff. Though it's very drinkable in summer.'

It was way too sweet for his taste, but he wasn't going to make her feel bad. 'It's fine.'

'Given that there were really only snacks at the danceathon, I ought to offer you a very late dinner,' she said, 'but I'm afraid all I have in my fridge is some salad, plus some ready-made pasta sauce and some dried pasta in the cupboard. And, especially as you're Italian and you're used to proper home-made pasta, I'm not sure I dare offer you that.'

Her kitchen didn't look like a cook's kitchen.

It looked more like the kind of place where she sat and chatted with friends, over coffee and cakes that she'd bought from the local bakery rather than made herself. There was a cork board on the wall with lots of leaflets pinned to it; dozens of photographs were held to the fridge with magnets, and he'd just bet the mantelpiece in her living room was crammed to bursting with photographs in frames.

'You've been literally rushed off your feet for the last six hours, not to mention setting up and clearing away again. I don't expect you to make dinner for me.' This was his perfect cue to go home.

Common sense said that he should go home. Now.

But part of him really wanted to stay. To get to know Jenna better.

He found himself saying, 'But I could cook for you, if you like.'

She blinked. 'Hang on. You're offering to cook for me?'

'I can't dance,' he said, 'but cooking's in my skill-set.'

'That's one up on me,' she said. 'My family always teases me that I could burn water. Lucy—my sister—insists on cooking for me on Monday nights so she knows I eat one proper meal a week.' She looked at him and frowned. 'You said your family owns a vine-yard. Do they own a restaurant as well?'

'Um, yes. Two or three. And a couple of hotels.'

She groaned. 'Then I am never, *ever* offering to cook for you.'

He laughed. 'Just because my cousin happens to be a Michelin-starred chef, it doesn't mean we're all that standard.'

She looked at him. 'Your cousin seriously has a Michelin star?'

'Yes. But Matteo's very down to earth,' Lorenzo protested. 'He just likes good, fresh food that's cooked well and presented well.'

She raised an eyebrow. 'I bet none of your family dares cook for him.'

'He's a chef, not a critic. If a meal is cooked for him with love, he'll eat it and smile, even if it's absolutely terrible.' Lorenzo grinned. 'Though the next morning whoever cooked it will get a quiet private lesson on how to make it better in future. Little tiny tweaks that you can remember easily and make a huge differ-ence to how edible the finished dish is. Mat-teo's one of the good guys.' He smiled. 'And he taught me to make great pasta sauce from just about anything.'

'Well, if you really want to see what you can do with an almost empty fridge, be my guest.' She spread her hands. 'But don't say I didn't warn you.'

'Let's have a look at what's there.' At her gesture of permission, he looked in her fridge. There was some olive oil margarine, cheese, some spring onions and tomatoes that were past their best, half a bag of tired-looking spinach, and a bulb of garlic that had started sprouting. Not brilliant, but he could work with it. And he wasn't going to use the jar of sauce, either.

'Do you have any fresh chilli?' he asked, though he was pretty sure he already knew the answer.

'Nope.' She rummaged in a cupboard. 'How about chilli flakes? I've never actually opened them. Lu probably bought them for me. Oh, wait…'

Lorenzo had to smother a grin as she checked the sell-by date and gave a visible sigh of relief. 'It's OK. They're still in date.'

'Good. All I need now is a sharp knife and

a chopping board, a grater, the pasta—oh, and two pans, please.'

A bit more rummaging in the cupboard, and she produced the dried pasta, a chopping board, a grater and two pans. 'The knife's in the drawer next to the sink. Don't you need the jar of sauce?'

'No,' he said with a smile. He put the kettle on to boil water for the pasta. 'We've got about ten minutes until dinner,' he said, once he'd poured the water over the pasta. 'Sit down and relax.' He grimaced. 'Sorry, I didn't mean to be bossy and take over. It's your kitchen.'

'It's fine,' she said. 'It's nice having my own personal chef.'

And actually it felt good to cook for someone again. He'd loved making pasta sauce for Florence, helping her feed herself and smiling as she smeared tomato sauce round her face and asked for more. *'Mato, Dada!'*

While the pasta bubbled away, he chopped the tomatoes, spring onions and garlic, added them to the pan with the margarine and sautéed them, then added the chilli flakes and the spinach to let the leaves wilt. Finally he grated the cheese.

Jenna had set the table while he was cooking; Lorenzo tested the pasta, then drained it and divided it between the two large pasta bowls she'd got ready, added the sauce, and sprinkled the cheese on top. 'Here we are.'

She took a mouthful and her eyes widened with pleasure, the way Florence's used to. 'I know what was in my fridge and I had no idea anyone could make anything from that lot, even Lu—and she loves cooking. This is seriously impressive. Did you ever think of being a chef, like your cousin?'

'No. I always wanted to be a doctor,' he said.

'Are either of your parents doctors?' she asked.

He shook his head. 'Dad's an architect and Mum works at the local nursery school. How about yours?'

'Dad's a GP and Mum's his practice nurse,' she said.

'Medicine runs in the family, then. So is your sister a medic, too?'

'No. Lucy is a primary school deputy head—one of the youngest to have the role,' she said, clearly very proud of her sister.

'What about you? Do you have brothers or sisters?'

'One of each—my brother's an architect, like my dad, and my sister's a florist. I'm the oldest.'

'Me, too,' she said with a smile. 'So does your cousin who's the chef live in London, too?'

'Verona,' Lorenzo explained. 'Most of my family live somewhere between the city and one of the towns on the southern end of Lake Garda, either working in the family vineyard or at the hotels or restaurants. My dad was the odd one out; he was always fascinated by buildings and he wanted to be an architect. Because he's the baby of the family, everyone supported him. They were really proud of him when he got a top job in London, even though it meant moving here and he wouldn't see much of everyone. Though obviously it's better nowadays with phones and video calls, and flights are so easy. We always spent the summer holidays at the vineyard when I was growing up and even during my student years, picking grapes and helping with the harvest. We'd take a boat out on the lake and have picnics after the day's work was done, and watch the sun set over the mountains.'

'That sounds idyllic,' she said.

'It was. Lake Garda's the most beautiful place on earth,' he said. 'Italy's my second home.'

'It sounds as if your family's close,' she said.

'They are.' Though he was the only one in his family who'd messed up his marriage. Both his brother and sister were happily married with a three-year-old each—exactly as he thought he'd be at this stage.

How wrong he'd been.

He looked at her. 'And, from the photographs on your fridge, so is yours.'

She smiled. 'We are.' She got up to take one of the photographs and handed it to him. 'That's Lucy, my brother-in-law Will, and their baby Ava. They would've been at the danceathon today—but Will's niece was getting married this afternoon, so they're up in Edinburgh for the weekend.'

He looked at the photograph and then back to her. 'Would I be right in saying Lucy's your identical twin?'

'Uh-huh. But I'm the oldest by a whole

three minutes.' She smiled. 'And I'm a very doting aunt. What about you? Do you have any nieces and nephews?'

'Yes.' *And, for eighteen months, I had a daughter. Except it was all a lie.* He shook himself. 'One of each. Riccardo has a little girl, Emily, and Chiara has a little boy, Jack. They're both three.' A couple of months older than Florence. 'And they both go to the nursery school where my mum works.'

'Oh, that's lovely.'

'It means they both settled in really quickly, because Nonna was there to make it familiar,' he said with a smile.

'Just like Lu takes Ava to Dad's surgery for vaccinations because Granny can always make Ava laugh and take her mind off the sting of the needle,' Jenna said.

There was something wistful in her face, quickly hidden again. But it felt too intrusive to ask.

He made polite conversation about food until they'd finished dinner.

'I'm sorry, I can't offer you pudding,' she said.

'That's fine. I'll wash up.'

She shook her head. 'You cooked, so I'll deal with the washing up.'

And now it really was his cue to leave. 'I guess I'd better let you get on. I'll see you at work on Monday, then.'

'Thank you for dinner,' she said.

He spread his hands. 'Hey, you provided the ingredients. I just cooked.'

'Half that stuff was well past its best and you still produced something amazing,' she pointed out.

'I like cooking. It relaxes me,' he said. And then curiosity got the better of him. 'What would you have done if I hadn't cooked?'

'Probably poured myself a bowl of cereal,' she admitted. 'Which is why Lu nags me.'

'I'd nag my sister, too, if she did that sort of thing,' he said. 'Actually, I nag her about breakfast all the time, because she's always up so early for the flower markets and she claims she doesn't have time to eat. Chiara would live on coffee if I didn't nag her.'

She smiled at him. 'Bossy oldest sibling, hmm?'

He laughed. 'And do you boss Lucy about?'

'Sometimes,' she admitted.

'There you are, then. Takes one to know one.'

She grinned. 'Bet I'm bossier than you.'

'You're definitely more of a hustler than me,' he said with a grin. 'Seriously, though, thanks for today. I really enjoyed it.' And he was surprised by how much fun it had been.

'And I really appreciate you giving up your time to help,' she said.

He accidentally brushed against her as she walked with him to her front door, and it sent a tingle right through him. It tipped him off balance to the point where he said, 'Maybe, if you're not busy tomorrow, I could take you out for lunch.'

Her eyes widened. 'That's very nice of you to ask me, and I'm flattered,' she said carefully, 'but I'm afraid I'm focusing solely on my exams right now. I'm not looking for a relationship.'

'Neither am I.' He blew out a breath. 'I'm sorry. I don't know why I just asked you out.' Honesty compelled him to add, 'There's just something about you that—I don't know. Draws me, I suppose.' And he wanted to move on, past the loneliness. He had a feeling that Jenna could be the one to help him do that.

Her face shuttered. 'I don't do relationships.'

Someone had obviously really, really hurt her. Time to back off. 'Then please forget I said anything. I'll let you get on.' He smiled at her. 'Goodnight, Jenna. See you at work on Monday.'

'Goodnight, Renzo. See you at work,' she said.

And he left before he could do something really stupid. Like giving in to the temptation to lean forward and kiss her.

CHAPTER FOUR

'AM I DOING the wrong thing, Charlie, turning Renzo down for a proper date?' Jenna asked, the next morning, as she was playing ball with her neighbour's dog in the park. 'I mean, I've known him for a couple of weeks. I've worked with him and I've seen for myself that he's great with patients, he's great with their parents, and he's really good with the junior staff on the ward, teaching them without making them feel stupid. He fits in well on team nights out. Plus he gave up all that time to help out at the danceathon yesterday. He's one of the good guys. I like him a lot. And he's drop-dead gorgeous. Half the women at the hospital would fall at his feet.'

The dog barked, and Jenna threw the tennis ball for him.

He retrieved it, scampered back and dropped it at her feet.

'But I haven't been asked out by anyone since—well, since Danny. And I got it so badly wrong with him. I thought we were getting on just fine. I thought we were happy. I thought he was going to ask me to marry him, and I was going to say yes. And then the adoption agency turned Lu down. It broke her heart. Of course I was going to offer to carry a baby for her. I wanted to make things right for her again.' She sighed. 'And Danny made it into something disgusting. Once he realised I really don't care about money, he accused me of fancying Will, and carrying the baby for Lu meant I was getting what I really wanted, having Will's baby. And it just wasn't true. I love Will dearly, but not in *that* way. He doesn't make my heart beat faster when he smiles. The room doesn't feel different when he walks in.'

Charlie tipped his head on one side, as if to say, 'Does the room feel different when Renzo walks in?'

That wasn't a question Jenna wanted to answer. Not right now. She threw the ball. 'I don't know if I can trust my judgement again, after Danny. I was so wrong about him. What if I've got it wrong about Renzo, too, and he's going to be just as disapproving and judgemental about the surrogacy?'

Charlie retrieved the tennis ball and deposited it at her feet.

'I know what Lu would say. He's a nice guy, so give him the benefit of the doubt. Talk to him.'

Charlie barked, as if agreeing.

'But it's not the easiest thing to talk about. What do I say? *Hey, before we start dating, just so you know, I was a surrogate mum for my twin sister's baby.*' She grimaced. 'It's not exactly the kind of thing you can just drop casually into a conversation, is it?'

Charlie cocked his head on one side, clearly waiting for her to throw the ball again.

Jenna threw it as hard as she could, and watched the dog run after it and bound back to her, his tail a blur. 'He asked me to have lunch with him. I said no. But I could call him, see if he's still free. Maybe we could go out as friends. See if we like each other enough to take it a step further. And if that does happen, then I'll work out how to tell him about Ava.'

Charlie brought the ball back and waited patiently for her to throw it

'I guess I just need to take life one step at a time instead of trying to plan it all in advance,' she said, and threw the ball. When the dog brought it back, she ruffled his fur and said, 'OK, sweetie. That's it for this morning. We need to get you back home to Evelyn.'

Charlie barked, as if to say, 'Just one more throw.'

How could she resist those adorable brown eyes?

Lorenzo's eyes were brown and adorable, too...

'How feeble am I, Charlie?' she asked ruefully, and threw the ball one last time. Then she made a fuss of the dog, stuffed the tennis ball in her coat pocket, clipped his lead back onto his collar and walked him back through the park to their street.

When she got back to her own house, she stared at her mobile phone. Lorenzo had given her his phone number before the danceathon, in case of emergency. Should she call him? Ask if his offer of lunch still stood?

It would be a risk. Opening herself up to rejection again.

But part of her knew she needed to move on from the past. Move on from the hurt Danny had caused her. And maybe Lorenzo was the one who could help her? Maybe she was the one who could help Lorenzo move on, too, from whatever had happened in his own past that put shadows in his eyes every so often?

There was only one way to find out.

She took a deep breath and called his number.

'Jenna,' he said when he answered. 'I wasn't expecting you to call me.'

'About yesterday,' she said. 'I was rude, and I apologise.'

'No, you were honest, and that's absolutely fine.'

'The thing is… I was wondering if you're still free for lunch? Because we could…' Her throat dried. 'Have lunch. As friends.' Oh, why was it so hard to get the words out? She sounded like an inarticulate teenager.

'Lunch as friends would be nice.'

'Not a date,' she checked.

'Not a date,' he agreed. 'Didn't you say you walk your neighbour's dog at weekends?'

'Yes, but I've already done that this morning.'

'Then we could meet at the tube station at, say, twelve,' he said.

'Twelve it is,' she said. 'See you there.'

And she ended the call before she could change her mind and make a fool of herself.

At twelve—after changing her mind half a dozen times about what she was going to wear, going from pretty dress to smart trousers to jeans and back again—Jenna met Lorenzo at the tube station. And her heart actually skipped a beat when she saw him in the distance and he smiled and raised his hand to tell her he'd seen her.

This could be really dangerous to her peace of mind. She hadn't reacted to anyone like this since Danny. But she knew she needed to put the past behind her. This was the first step.

'How was your dog-walk?' Lorenzo asked when she reached him.

'Half of it was playing ball in the park, so Charlie—that's the dog—did most of the work, running to fetch it and bring it back to me,' she said with a smile. 'But I think I've worn him out for Evelyn—my neighbour—so he'll sleep for most of the afternoon now.'

'It's nice of you to walk him for her.'

'It's not just me. I have a rota with four of

my neighbours,' she explained. 'I do week-ends, because I don't have children or any urgent calls on my time if I'm not at work, and the others do either the morning or evening walks during the week. We're all really happy to do it, because it means Evelyn doesn't have to give up her dog now her arthritis has made her too frail to walk him properly herself—that would've broken her heart. Plus we all get to enjoy having a part-time dog without worrying or feeling guilty about having to leave him alone at home all day while we're at work. And it's a really good excuse for us to be able to keep an eye on Evelyn and make sure she's all right, without stripping her of her dignity or her independence.'

'It sounds like a nice community.'

'It is,' she agreed. Everyone had kept an eye out for her, too, when she'd been pregnant with Ava. Not that she was ready to tell Lorenzo about that. Not just yet.

'So what made you change your mind?' he asked.

'About lunch? I was hungry.'

He simply looked at her, and she grimaced. 'OK. What you said last night—when you said there was something about me...' She stumbled over the words. 'Maybe there's something about you that draws me, too. But I have to be honest. This whole thing scares me. I wasn't looking for a relationship.'

'You're not alone,' he said. 'I wasn't looking for a relationship, either. And this scares me as much as I think it scares you.'

She took a deep breath. 'I'm guessing someone hurt you. And I'm not going to push you to talk about it.'

He nodded. 'I'm guessing someone hurt you, too. And I'm also guessing that what you just said means you don't want to talk about it, either.'

'Correct.' She wasn't ready to tell him about Ava, but she could tell him about Danny. 'Bare bones—I picked the wrong guy and he gave me an ultimatum. It was an easy choice. But I was pretty shocked he'd taken that attitude. He wasn't the man I thought I'd fallen in love with, so I don't trust my judgement any more.'

Ultimatum. Maybe he'd got it wrong about her possibly taking a sabbatical for a pregnancy and then losing a baby, Lorenzo thought. But what kind of man would give

an ultimatum to a woman like Jenna? OK, so
he didn't know her that well, and she could
have a massive character flaw—but he didn't
think so. Her ex sounded like a control freak.

To reassure her, Lorenzo said, 'Just so you
know, I don't do ultimatums.' And, because
she'd shared a confidence, he felt he ought to
do the same. Not the whole messy story, but
enough for her to know that he too had picked
the wrong one for him. 'My ex-wife,' he said,
'left me for the love of her life.' Which he'd
thought was him. How wrong he'd been. He
didn't want to tell Jenna the rest of it—he
didn't want to face the kind of pity that had
soured his shifts at the London Victoria—but
maybe this way she wouldn't feel so alone.

And it felt strangely healing to say it out
loud: that Georgia had left him for the man
she really loved. That she'd married him without really meaning her vows. That she hadn't
loved him as much as he'd loved her.

'So we've both made mistakes,' she said.
'And learned from them.' She looked at him,
her eyes very blue. 'So. No pity.'

'No pity,' he agreed.

'And we'll see how things go,' she said.
'No promises.'

'That sounds good to me. Where would you like to go for lunch?'

'That depends. I was thinking,' she said, 'maybe we could do something after lunch, too.'

He smiled. 'I'd like that. Do you have something particular in mind?'

'Yes. But I need to ask you first—seeing as your dad's an architect, does that mean you love buildings or they bore you to tears?' she asked.

'I love them,' he said.

She looked pleased. 'I was hoping you'd say that. How would you like to go and visit the ruins of a Roman bath house that are usually hidden from view?'

He blinked at her. 'A Roman bath house? Hang on. My family's Italian, and I've spent most of my life in London. How come I've never heard of this Roman bath house before?'

She wrinkled her nose. 'It's in the basement of a building, and I don't think it's had very much publicity. But they do tours. I could see if I can book us tickets for this afternoon, if you like.'

'I'd like that.'

She grabbed her phone and found the website, then went through to the ticket-booking section. 'We're in luck—they have spaces in the two o'clock tour today, which means we have time for lunch first. Monument's our nearest Tube station, though we're getting in at Moorgate and it's only a few minutes' walk from there.'

'Walking sounds fine,' he said, and she booked the tickets.

'How much do I owe you for my ticket?' he asked. 'Or can I buy us both lunch on the grounds that you bought the tickets?'

'Lunch would be nice,' she said. 'I've no idea where, though. Do you happen to know that bit of the city very well?'

'Not really. I know South Bank better, and obviously Victoria because I worked there for years,' he said. 'So either we need to look up a few reviews while we're on the train, or we have a wander round when we get there and find somewhere with a menu we like the look of.'

'My vote's for wandering round,' she said promptly.

'Mine, too.'

It was too noisy on the train to chat much

on the way in, but once they'd got to Moorgate and were walking through the city, it
was easy to talk.

'That's amazing,' he said, gesturing up to
the enormous white column looming above
the streets in front of them. 'I know it's daft,
considering how famous it is, but I've never
actually seen the Monument for myself. I had
no idea it was that tall or the gold urn at the
top was so bright.'

'I've been this close to it before, but never
actually climbed it,' Jenna admitted. 'The
views from the platform at the top are meant
to be amazing.'

'Maybe,' he said, 'we could do that some
time.'

'We could make a list of the touristy things
we'd like to do in London but we've never actually done because we live here and take it
all for granted,' she suggested.

'Great idea. Let's start the list over lunch,'
he said.

They wandered round the streets, looking
at the menus in the windows of all the restaurants.

'This one looks good,' he said.

Jenna checked the dessert menu, and smiled

with pleasure. 'Salted caramel profiteroles—
my favourite. Oh, yes. I agree. Let's go here.'

'Do you always read menus backwards?'
he asked.

'Yup. If I love all the puddings, then I'll
choose a restrained main course. If I'm not
that fussed about the puddings, then I'll have
a larger main instead,' she said.

'That works for me, too,' he said.

Once they were settled at their table, Jenna
ordered smoked salmon fishcakes with a
green salad, and Lorenzo chose ale-glazed
chicken with mashed potato, green beans and
heirloom tomatoes. And both of them ordered
profiteroles.

The food was good, but the salted caramel
profiteroles were outstanding.

'Utterly gorgeous,' Jenna said after her last
mouthful. 'This was an excellent idea.'

After Florence had been born, Georgia had
become really fussy about food, convinced
that she needed to lose weight when she was
perfectly fine as she was. It was a really nice
change to have lunch with someone who enjoyed what they ate, Lorenzo thought. True,
Jenna had asked the waitress to swap the

sweet potato fries for a green salad, but her order had been made with the profiteroles in mind. For her it was about balance rather than self-sacrifice.

With Georgia, after Florence's birth, nothing had seemed to be right. He'd tried to be patient, and he'd talked in confidence to an obstetrician friend about the possibility of postnatal depression and how to help her. And all the time he'd had no idea what was wrong. She wouldn't tell him, and he hadn't been able to reassure her that whatever it was he would be there and they could work it out together.

When she'd finally told him about Scott, everything had fallen into place.

He'd felt so betrayed. She'd cheated on him and she'd married him without really loving him. It had taken him quite a while to come to terms with that.

Finding out that Florence wasn't his daughter had been hard, but he could've dealt with that. He'd fallen in love with the baby the second that he'd first held her. Even if he'd had a rough day at work, going home would make things all right in his world because he knew she'd beam at him the moment he walked in the door, holding her chubby arms up to him in a demand to be picked up. 'Dada' had even been her first word. He'd adored her, and she'd loved him all the way back. Finding out that he wasn't actually her biological father had made no difference to his feelings about Florence. She was still *his* daughter, in his eyes.

And losing her had made him feel as if he'd been dropped down a deep, dark well.

He'd tried to tell himself that Georgia was doing the right thing, making a family with Scott—her ex and Florence's natural father. And of course there could be no room for Lorenzo in that family. It would be way too confusing for the little girl, not knowing who to call 'daddy': the man who'd brought her up for the first eighteen months of her life, or the man who was her biological father and now lived with her mother. Plus Georgia and Scott had moved to Birmingham, too far for Lorenzo to drop in to see Florence after work on a weekday.

Lorenzo just hoped that Scott really *had* changed. That he wasn't going to drift back into his old ways and end up back in prison. That he'd be a proper father to Florence, loving her and protecting her from any hurt,

splashing about in a swimming pool with her
and telling her bedtime stories—the kind of
father Lorenzo had been to her.

His parents, too, had been desperately hurt
at losing one of their three grandchildren.
But Georgia had insisted on a clean break.
A break that had left Lorenzo with nothing.
No closure.

There had been no chance for him to fight
Georgia for custody, because the DNA test
proved that Florence wasn't his. Plus his name
wasn't on the birth certificate: Georgia had
said she'd get it changed once they were married, but she hadn't got round to it. Probably
because she'd always guessed that he wasn't
Florence's father—Florence had Scott's grey
eyes and red hair rather than Lorenzo's dark
eyes and hair—and Lorenzo had tried to tell
himself that at least Georgia had been honest in that respect and hadn't lied on the birth
certificate.

But, oh, how he missed his little girl. How
he missed being a dad. How he missed the
closeness of living with a family.

'Are you OK?' Jenna asked as they reached
Billingsgate.

He forced himself to smile. The wreckage

of his life wasn't Jenna's fault, and he didn't want to dump his feelings on her. 'Sure. I was just wool-gathering. Sorry.'

'No problem. We're meant to meet the tour guide just here,' she said, indicating a very plain and modern-looking building.

Once the group was gathered together, the guide led them inside the building and down a flight of steps to the basement. And there in the centre of the floor was the base of a Roman bath house, with a hypocaust system and arches showing where the furnaces once were.

The guide talked them through the different areas of the bath house.

'So the caldarium was the bit like a modern sauna, the tepidarium was the largest room where they had all the treatments in a nice warm area, including having hairs plucked out, and the frigidarium was the bit where they closed their pores in a freezing bath— well, in this case, there wasn't room to build a plunge pool, so the bathers dipped into the water tank at the end of the frigidarium,' Jenna said.

'All that oil being scraped off with strigils, and bits of hair everywhere—can you imagine how vile the floor of the tepidarium would be at the end of the day?' Lorenzo asked with a grin.

'Ah, but as the rich young man who was being scraped off and depilated, you wouldn't care—because you wouldn't be the one to clean it up,' she retorted, laughing.

'It's strange. In Italy, you're used to the ancient buildings being scattered around the city on full view,' Lorenzo said. 'You've got the Arena in Verona, then all the buildings of the Forum and the Colosseum in Rome. I thought in London all that was left of the Roman settlement was a bit of the old boundary wall.'

'There are quite a few more bits of wall left than you'd think there are; it's just that a lot of them are hidden away underneath or inside newer buildings,' Jenna said. 'The Roman settlement here was totally deserted after the Romans left, and everything just collapsed in on itself. It wasn't rediscovered for years—or, rather, it was just ignored until the ground was cleared and new footings were dug and then the remains were rediscovered. There's an amphitheatre under the Guildhall, there's a temple of Mithras that ended up being moved so people could see the ruins properly, and there's a Roman ditch and pavement in the crypt at St Bride's church, just off Fleet Street. Oh, and there's another Roman pavement in the crypt at All Hallows, next to the Tower of London.'

Lorenzo was impressed by her knowledge. 'How do you know all this stuff, Jenna?'

'That's the thing about having a nerdy history professor for a brother-in-law,' she said with a smile. 'Will's specialist subject is Roman Britain, and he does quite a few field trips with his students. Before he plans a new field trip, Lucy and I get to do a trial run with him. So I've been to every fort on Hadrian's Wall and walked quite a lot of the route, too. And I'm pretty sure Will's actually worked out a walk so you can see every bit of the old Roman wall here in London. I can ask him, if you'd like to do that.'

'So you've obviously been here before?'

'With Will and Lucy,' she confirmed. 'So I know the floor here has tesserae but it wasn't an actual mosaic floor—say, like the amazing ones at the palace in Fishbourne—and archaeologists are never really going to be able to prove whether this was a private house or an inn, because what we can see of the ruins is bounded by the Thames on one side and the roadway on another and there isn't quite enough evidence to say either way.'

'Fair point,' he said. 'So you bonded with your brother-in-law over history?'

She nodded. 'I really thought about becoming a forensic archaeologist, when I was in my teens. But then I did work experience on a dig in Northumbria, the summer I was waiting for my exam results, and I realised that as an archaeologist I was going to spend a lot of my working life kneeling in mud under a leaking tarpaulin in the rain. That wasn't what I wanted. So I switched to living patients rather than dead ones.' She smiled. 'But whenever I go on a city break, the first place I check out is the museum. Luckily Lu feels the same way that I do about history—that's how she met Will.'

'In a museum?'

'Planning a trip on Roman London for her Year Six class,' Jenna explained. 'A friend of a friend suggested that she talked to Will. So they met at the British Museum one Saturday morning for an hour's chat, and they were still there at closing time. Six months later, I was walking down the aisle behind her, carrying

Lu's train and holding her bouquet at the aisle while she and Will plighted their troth.'

'That's nice,' Lorenzo said, meaning it. His own siblings were happily married, and it was good to hear of relationships that had worked. Not everyone's was a failure, the way his had been.

'Everyone likes Will. He's a sweetie. Though he does like doing the vague professor thing, which drives me crazy.' She rolled her eyes. 'Lu has to tell him they're meeting friends an hour before they really are meeting up, otherwise they'd always be late.'

'Is your twin like you?' Lorenzo asked.

'Organised and a hustler? Put it this way, she's the deputy head at her primary school. So among other things she needs to be incredibly organised, juggle budgets and support the PTA in fundraising.' Jenna wrinkled her nose. 'But I think she's nicer than I am—plus she can cook.'

Cooking was optional, in Lorenzo's view. As for nice: the more he talked to Jenna, the more he liked her.

Was she the one who could teach him to trust again?

When their tour was over, they headed back out into the sunshine.

'I happen to know somewhere else really nice just round the corner from here,' Jenna said. 'You said you didn't know this bit of the city. Shall we do some exploring?'

'Sure.'

She took him round the corner to what looked like a church—until he noticed that it was roofless, there was ivy growing over the walls and there was no glass in the windows.

The plaque on the wall told him that the church of St Dunstan's in the East was rebuilt by Wren after the Great Fire of London; it was bombed in the Blitz but Wren's tower remained and the church area was made into a garden.

'So just over there we have all the hustle and bustle of the City of London,' Lorenzo said. 'And here it's just peace and calm, full of flowers and bees.'

'Amazing, isn't it?' Jenna said. 'I came here with Will and Lu, too. She used it as inspiration when they started building the sensory garden at her school.'

'I can see why,' Lorenzo said.

There were several wooden benches arranged around the small bubbling foundation in the centre of the church floor. They sat on one of the spare benches and watched the bees hovering over the flowers of the shrubs planted in the garden.

'The perfect English summer day,' Jenna said.

'Maybe there was a garden here in Roman times, too,' Lorenzo said. 'Just round the corner from the bath house.'

'A walled one, to help shelter from the cold in winter,' she said. 'No wonder they needed the underfloor heating in that Roman house. I still can't imagine how cold it must've been back then for the Thames to freeze over.'

'Especially on a warm summer day like this one,' Lorenzo agreed.

As they left the church grounds, their hands accidentally brushed against each other again. Lorenzo gave in to the impulse to let his fingers link with Jenna's. She didn't pull away, and they walked in silence back towards the Monument, hand in hand. Oddly, this felt *right*.

'Maybe,' he suggested, 'we could walk by the river for a bit.'

'I'd like that,' she said. 'From here, we could

walk down to Tower Bridge, then head over the river to the South Bank.'

'That'd be good.'

He held her hand all the way along the side of the Thames and across the bridge. And somehow they were still holding hands by the time they got to the South Bank. There were street entertainers, stalls selling everything from jewellery and crafts through to books and prints. Children were darting in and out of the fountain installations, laughing. Something he'd enjoyed doing with Florence, as soon as she was old enough to toddle. He'd lifted her over the walls of water and she'd giggled and clapped her hands. *'Uv oo, Dada.'*

Gone.

All gone.

Something had put the sadness back in Lorenzo's face, Jenna thought. What was it about the South Bank that had made him feel that way? She loved the vibrancy of the area, the street entertainers and the art installations. And she'd always loved the fountains.

On impulse, she tugged at his hand. 'Come on. Let's get to the other side of the fountain rooms. The one who gets wettest buys the drinks.'

At that, the shadow seemed to clear from his face. 'OK. You're on.'

Lorenzo was the first to get sprayed by the fountain when a mini wall of water sprang up unexpectedly.

Jenna, halfway across the installation and still completely dry, grinned. 'Oh, dear. Poor Renzo. You are so buying those drinks.'

'Don't bet on it,' he teased back.

She was just about to be smug and step out onto the other side of the installation when she realised she'd misjudged her timing—and was promptly soaked by the largest wall of water popping up.

Lorenzo strolled across when the water had died down again. 'You were saying, Dr Harris?'

'All right, so the drinks are on me,' she said, giving a mock pained sigh. 'Do you want beer, wine or coffee?'

'Actually, the smoothies over there look good,' he said, indicating one of the stalls.

'Smoothies it is, then,' she said with a smile.

Once she'd bought their smoothies, they

sat on one of the benches overlooking the Thames, watching the light playing on the water and looking over at the buildings on the North Bank, from the glass and steel constructions of the buildings in the City of London through to the towering dome of St Paul's. She felt Lorenzo shift slightly next to her, and then his arm slid round her shoulders.

They'd held hands. This was the next logical step. If she pulled away, she knew without having to ask that he'd respect her boundaries and give her space.

The problem was, she didn't want to pull away.

So she shifted slightly, too, moving closer to him. And in response his arm tightened slightly round her.

It was so easy to be with Lorenzo. Jenna didn't feel that she had to chatter to fill the space. It was fine just sitting together in the sunshine, sipping smoothies and watching the world go by. She couldn't remember the last time she'd done something like this, and it made her ache.

When they walked to the Tube station, their arms were still wrapped round each other.

Lorenzo held her hand on the train and all the way back to her flat.

Butterflies were doing a stampede in her stomach, a mixture of excitement and fear.

What now?

She turned to him, intending to kiss him on the cheek and thank him for a lovely day. And somehow she missed and her mouth brushed against his. Her lips tingled where they touched his, and the tingle ran all the way down to the base of her spine.

Knowing she shouldn't be doing this, she did it again. And this time his arms wrapped round her and he deepened the kiss.

Kissing like a teenager on her front doorstep.

How long had it been since she'd done something like this? Years and years and years.

She pulled back slightly and looked him straight in the eye. 'Sorry. That wasn't supposed to happen.'

'No need to apologise.' He rested his palm lightly against her cheek and stroked the pad of his thumb over her lower lip. 'But it did happen. So what now?'

'We both said we weren't in a place where

we wanted a relationship,' she reminded him. 'That we'd just see how things go.'

'True,' he said. 'But this thing between us—somehow I don't think this is going to be easy to ignore.'

'Also true,' she said. 'But you and I—I think we both come with baggage.'

'Stuff that's been hard to deal with, and just as hard to talk about.' He looked at her. 'So we'll be kind to each other. No pressure. No promises. Just enjoy each other's company.'

Friends, but with the possibility of more. Not rushing into things. 'Taking it slowly,' she said, 'sounds good.'

He leaned forward and kissed her again. This time it was very deliberate and it made her knees feel as if they'd melted.

'See you tomorrow,' he said.

'Tomorrow,' she echoed.

And Monday suddenly looked as if it was going to be very bright indeed.

CHAPTER FIVE

AT WORK THE next day, Jenna and Lorenzo were both busy in the PAU. It seemed to be Jenna's day for sorting out fractures: a girl who'd fallen over roller-skating and put her hands out to save herself, ending up with a greenstick fracture of her arm; a boy who'd fallen off the monkey bars in the playground and fractured his elbow; and a toddler who'd fallen over while running around at playgroup and ended up with a spiral fracture of his tibia.

'Got time for lunch before your next clinic?' Lorenzo asked as they headed out to the staff kitchen.

'Lunch would be great. I could really do with some coffee,' Jenna said feelingly. 'It's been one of those mornings.'

'Rough cases?' he asked.

'Fractures, fractures and more fractures,' she said.

'Don't tell me. Greenstick ulnar fractures?'

She grimaced. 'One, plus a spiral tibia—though the one that worries me is the lad who fell off the monkey bars.'

'Supracondylar fracture?' Lorenzo asked.

Breaking an arm just above the elbow was one of the most common fractures in children, so it was a fair guess. 'No. This one was actually on the joint. I had to send him up for surgery.'

Lorenzo winced. 'Poor lad. Was it a simple fracture or has he injured the growth plate as well?'

'Right now, I don't know. We'll need to keep an eye on him,' she said. 'How about you? How was your morning?'

'Full of small children with rashes, along with mums who were in a bit of a panic,' he said. 'Thankfully none of them turned out to be septicaemia. I've put one toddler on a food exclusion diet, though, to see if it helps with her eczema. Her mum's already using non-bio washing powder and being careful with detergents and toiletries, so we agreed to look at foods, and we're following up in a fortnight.'

'Starting with dairy?' she asked.

He nodded. 'The usual suspects. I gave the mum a list of substitutes—she was already clued up about caring for sore, itchy skin and she's using the right emollients.'

'It's tough for parents, isn't it?'

'Yes.'

There was another shadow in his face, quickly masked, and Jenna was starting to wonder. She knew that his wife had left him for someone else, but she had a feeling there was more to it than that—just as there was to her situation with Danny. Had they maybe lost a child, first, and the only way his ex had been able to cope was to find someone else, someone who hadn't shared the pain with her and reminded her of the loss every time she saw him? In which case, working on the paediatric ward must be so difficult for him — or maybe he was such a dedicated doctor precisely because he knew how it felt to have a sick child and he wanted to spare other people going through the same pain.

Though asking him straight out felt much too intrusive. Until he was ready to talk to her, she wouldn't pry. Especially because she wasn't enough of a hypocrite to expect him to open up about his past without admitting to her own.

Awkwardly, she changed the subject. 'I'm ordering toys this weekend. I have a wish-list going round the ward for suggestions so, if you have any strong views on what we need, make sure you grab the list.'

'I will.' He smiled at her. 'Can I take you out to dinner tonight?'

'Sorry. Mondays are my evening with Lucy, Will and Ava.'

'Tomorrow?'

She shook her head. 'Tuesday is salsa class.' She smiled back. 'You could come to salsa class with me, if you like, and we could grab something to eat afterwards.'

'Thanks for the offer, but my two left feet are already wincing at the idea of more salsa. Wednesday's the team ten-pin bowling night out,' he said.

'And Thursday is my ballroom class. So maybe we can do something on Friday?' she suggested.

'Friday it is,' he agreed.

When they walked through the reception

area back towards the ward, Jenna noticed there was a table with a bake sale in aid of dementia patients.

'Hang on a sec,' she said, and browsed the table for a couple of minutes before buying a coffee and walnut cake.

'Is that for the ward kitchen?' he asked.

'No, it's for my sister tonight. Coffee and walnut cake is her absolute favourite.'

'Then I'll buy some cake for the ward kitchen,' he said, and chose a lemon drizzle cake.

'I would've pegged you as a chocolate cake fiend,' she said.

'Pretty much any cake will do,' he said, 'but lemon drizzle cake has always been my favourite. My mother puts limoncello in hers.'

'Would that be limoncello made by your family, from your own lemon orchard?' she asked.

'Actually, yes, it would.' He laughed. 'We're terribly clichéd. Wine, lemons—the only thing we don't grow right now is olives, though I think one of my cousins is eyeing up a grove or two and thinking about branching out. Pun most definitely not intended,' he added with a grin.

'It's nice that you're kind of the bedrock of the local economy,' she said. 'Lu's very keen on all the slow food stuff.'

'Good food is always worth paying attention to,' he said.

'You sound like my twin,' she said with a smile. Lorenzo and Lucy would get on really well, she was sure. But she wasn't ready to introduce him to her family just yet. They'd agreed to take it slowly and see where things took them. And that suited her just fine.

That evening, Jenna skilfully used cake to deflect Lucy's questions about the danceathon, and turned the conversation to the wedding in Scotland. She knew if she admitted that she was seeing Lorenzo, Lucy would insist on meeting him, checking him out to make sure he wasn't another Danny. And then the grilling would begin—for both of them. She wasn't ready to talk, yet, even to her twin.

Yes, she'd like to be as happy and Lucy and Will were. But where did you find somebody to love, somebody who'd love you all the way back? In your thirties, anyone you met had baggage. Cracks in their heart from previous relationships. Could she and Lorenzo heal each other's hearts, or would their new relationship fall through those cracks?

On Wednesday night, Lorenzo and Jenna were both at the ward's ten-pin bowling night out, though they were on different teams and didn't get much chance to talk to each other. But on Thursday evening Lorenzo was browsing through the local 'what's on' website and spotted something he liked the look of: Screen under the Stars. He really liked the idea of seeing a film outdoors.

Even though he knew Jenna was at her dance class, he sent her a text, knowing she'd pick it up at some point later that evening.

Pop-up cinema in the park tomorrow evening. Weather forecast good. Shall we?

As he'd hoped, she texted back after her class.

Love to. What's the film?

Dirty Dancing.

Excellent choice :) What time?

Meet you at your place at seven?

Perfect.

They were both too busy even to grab a cup of coffee together, the next day. But at seven that evening, he rang her doorbell.

'What's that?' she asked, nodding at the large bag he was carrying.

'A fleecy blanket,' he said. 'It'll be cold when the sun goes down, even though it's June.'

'Good thinking,' she said. 'Shall I go and dig out my fold-up picnic chairs?'

'No need,' he said with a smile, 'because our tickets are the VIP ones that include chairs.'

'Excellent organisation on your part, Dr Conti,' she said, and slid her arm round his waist. 'And, because you bought the tickets, I'm buying the drinks and nibbles.'

'Fine by me,' he said.

They walked to the park together, queued up so their tickets could be scanned from his phone, bought drinks and popcorn, and then went to find their chairs.

'I really love this film,' Jenna said with a smile.

'So Patrick Swayze's your ideal man?' he asked.

'Dancing like that? You bet!' She wrinkled her nose. 'Though really it's the way he sticks up for Baby at the end that I like most. It's important for your partner to fight your corner.'

'Rather than giving you an ultimatum.' The words were out before he could stop them, and he winced. 'Sorry.'

'No, you're right.' She sighed. 'Danny didn't agree with me taking a sabbatical.' She looked torn, as if she wanted to tell him more but something was holding her back.

She'd told him that she didn't trust her own judgement any more. So he simply took her hand. 'I'm assuming you had a good reason. It's a shame he didn't support you.'

'He said it was career suicide. That I could never make up the lost money and promotions.' She dragged in a breath. 'But some things are more important than money.'

Was this time she'd taken to have a child—and perhaps lost the baby and Danny hadn't been there for her? Though he could hardly ask.

'From what I see, you're a well-respected member of the team. He was wrong about a sabbatical being career suicide. Doctors do it all the time. Some to work for Doctors Without Borders, others take parental leave, others need to look after a sick relative for a while. Life happens. You didn't make the wrong choice.'

'Thank you,' she said.

Her ex sounded incredibly selfish. No wonder she didn't trust her judgement, if she'd fallen in love with someone like that. 'No problem,' he said softly.

Lorenzo held her hand all the way through the film and just enjoyed the movie.

As the sun finished setting, he noticed that Jenna was shivering slightly, so he tucked the blanket round her and went to fetch hot chocolate and hot dogs to warm them up.

'Thank you,' she said, and kissed him lightly. 'It's nice to have someone make a fuss of me.'

Clearly her ex hadn't done that, and he knew what it felt like to choose the wrong partner. But he didn't want to talk about that, either, so he just smiled. 'My pleasure.'

There was something special about watching a film under the stars, and Lorenzo enjoyed every second of it.

'So would you do a lift like that one in your ballroom class?' he asked as they walked back to her place after the movie had ended.

'I guess some choreographers might put it into a show dance,' she said, 'but to be honest we don't tend to do lifts when we go through routines or learn new steps. I'm not in the advanced class.'

'The way you were dancing at the danceathon looked pretty advanced to me.'

She shook her head. 'Those were really just easy basics. If you put a few of them together in a combination, the routine looks a lot more flashy and complicated than it really is.'

Back at her flat, he kissed her goodnight on the doorstep. 'Can I see you tomorrow?' he asked. 'I could cook dinner for you.'

She looked pleased by the idea. 'Thanks. I'd like that.'

'Good. Is there anything you don't eat?'

'I like everything,' she said. 'Except maybe not lasagne, because my sister's lasagne is the best in the world—and, yes, I know your cousin has a Michelin star, but I still stand by my opinion and I reckon her lasagne could hold its own against his.'

For a moment, he wondered if she was going to suggest meeting her family. But this was still very early days. He wasn't sure he was ready for her to meet his family yet, either. 'Fair enough.' He kissed her again, then told her his address. 'Is seven o'clock OK?'

'That's fine. See you then. And thank you again for a really lovely evening.'

'My pleasure.' He stole a last kiss. 'See you tomorrow.'

'I think I've made the right decision, Charlie,' Jenna told the dog when they went to the park the next morning. 'Lorenzo's really lovely—and yes, he does make the room feel different when he walks in.' She ruffled the dog's fur. 'But we're taking it slowly, just getting to know each other. I know I have to tell him about Ava, but…' She wrinkled her nose. 'Maybe not just yet.'

Once she'd delivered Charlie back home and made Evelyn a cup of tea, she headed to the shops to find something nice to take with her that evening. She browsed in the local chocolatier's and found something she hoped would be perfect, then bought a couple of bottles of wine from the posher shelves at the supermarket. After giving Charlie his second, shorter walk of the day, she went home to shower, wash her hair and change into a dress.

At seven precisely, she stood on Lorenzo's doorstep and rang the bell.

He answered immediately. 'Hello.'

He was wearing a smart casual shirt and chinos, and looked utterly edible. Her pulse speeded up a notch.

Though he'd invited her for dinner and she couldn't actually smell anything cooking…

The doubts must've shown in her face, because he said, 'I've done all the prep for dinner, but it takes just ten minutes to cook, and I've cheated with the bread and bought the sort you just heat through in the oven—because my bread-making is on about a par with my dancing.'

Jenna liked his honesty. Danny would've bluffed his way through it and made out that he'd been slaving away in the kitchen all day. Danny liked to impress; 'my girlfriend, the doctor' brought him kudos, in his eyes, whereas 'my girlfriend, the surrogate mum' most definitely hadn't.

She pushed the thought away and smiled. 'You're still one up on me, because I can burn water, remember?'

'Hmm.'

Lorenzo kissed her hello, and even though it was a relatively chaste kiss it still made her knees go weak. She hadn't felt like this about anyone since she was a teenager, and it was scary and exciting at the same time.

'I forgot to ask you if I should bring red or white wine, so I played it safe.' She handed him a bottle of each.

'You really didn't need to do that.'

'Yes, I did—it's my contribution to tonight. Oh. And this.' She handed him a box of *gianduja*. 'Though it kind of feels a bit cheeky, giving Italian chocolates to an Italian.'

'Not at all. These are my absolute favourites. *Mille grazie*. Thank you very much.'

Oh, she loved it when he spoke Italian. So *sexy*.

He kissed her again. 'I hope you don't mind eating in the kitchen, but I don't have a separate dining room.'

'It's fine,' she said. 'And I get to watch you cook, so it counts as dinner and a show, right?'

He laughed. 'Now you've said that, I can definitely do you a show. I have a whole range of terrible jokes, half of which were taught to me by seven-year-olds.'

She laughed back. 'I bet they're very similar to the ones that some seven-year-old patients taught me. Which means they're really terrible.'

'Let's see. Why did the bicycle lean against the wall?' he asked.

She grinned. 'Because it was two-tyred. Actually, that's one of my favourites.' She paused. 'I have one for you. Knock, knock.'

'Who's there?'

'Cows go.'

'Cows go who?' he asked.

'No, silly. Cows go moo.'

He groaned. 'That's absolutely awful!' Then his gorgeous brown eyes crinkled at the corners and her knees went weak again. 'I'll remember that, next time I have a patient who's scared of needles and needs distracting. Thank you.' He ushered her into the kitchen. 'Can I get you a drink?'

'Yes, please. Whatever's open,' she said.

He took a bottle from the fridge, poured her a glass, and gestured to her to sit at the table.

'This is really nice,' she said after the first sip. 'I assume it's a Conti family wine?'

'Yes. It's the *chiaretto*. Actually, I helped pick the grapes for this particular vintage.'

'There aren't many people who can say that about the wine they drink,' she said.

There were two chopping boards on the worktop next to the cooker, one with a pile of chopped vegetables and one with a pile of what looked like chopped scallops. There were a couple of saucepans on the hob, a jug of stock and a couple of bowls with ingredients in.

'Are you hungry? Is it OK for me to start cooking?' he asked.

'Sounds perfect,' she said with a smile. 'I would ask if there was anything I can do, but it's probably safer for me to sit here and let you do the magical stuff.'

'No problem.' He glanced at his watch, then poured boiling water over the pasta; next, he switched on the oven and put the bread in to heat through; and finally he heated butter and began to sauté the chopped garlic and onions. Within two minutes, the kitchen smelled heavenly. Lorenzo was a very deft cook, but Jenna had already seen the way he'd worked in her own kitchen, so she knew what to expect.

'So is this one of your cousin's recipes?' she asked.

'It's the family version,' he said. 'The one Matteo would cook in his restaurant is a bit more complicated, plus he'd do all the flashy plating with pretty dabs of sauce. Which, by the way, you won't get from me.'

'That's fine. I already know from what you did in my kitchen that you're a good cook. You don't need to pretty up the food on my behalf,' she said. She watched Lorenzo sauté the chopped courgettes and scallops; then he added stock, saffron and sun-dried tomatoes.

'That smells amazing,' she said.

'It's one of my favourite sauces,' he said.

He checked his watch, then added a spoonful of crème fraîche to the sauce. Then he drained the pasta, mixed in the sauce and divided it between two bowls, took the bread from the oven, and served up.

'I've never seen pasta like this before,' she said, looking at the short, fat, ridged tubes. 'Lucy likes messing about with different pasta shapes, but even she hasn't cooked me this before.'

'It's *pacchieri*,' he said. 'The shape and the ridges mean it holds the sauce better.'

'Right.' She took a mouthful. 'Wow. This tastes even better than it smells.'

'Thank you—but you saw for yourself, it really wasn't that difficult to make. All you do is follow a recipe, just like you follow the procedures for treating a medical condition.'

'Nope, not convinced,' she said. 'This is wonderful. Between you and Lucy, I've eaten really well this week.'

'What, no bowls of cereal for dinner?' he teased.

'Twice, this week,' she said. 'After salsa and ballroom class. But I'll have you know it's seriously good granola, and I added blueberries and banana and Greek yoghurt—so it was pretty healthy.'

'I'll teach you a couple of easy recipes,' he said.

'Thanks for the offer, but Lu's already tried and failed. I'm much better at appreciating food than cooking it, and I'm happy to stay that way,' she said.

'Fair enough.'

After they'd finished the pasta, he cleared their empty plates away and brought over a bowl of strawberries, then a plate of shortbread and a tub of premium vanilla ice cream.

'The strawberries look nice,' she said.

'I've done them the Italian way, sliced thickly and marinated in balsamic vinegar, sugar and black pepper for thirty minutes at room temperature.'

She raised an eyebrow. 'Black pepper, with strawberries? Seriously?'

'Seriously. It brings out the flavour. Give it a try.'

She did. 'You're right. It really brings out the flavour. And that shortbread is fantastic. If you make some of that for the ward kitchen, you'll have everyone worshipping you.'

He laughed. 'It's not *that* difficult to make. Maybe we can cook some together, at some point.'

'Maybe,' she said, her tone making it clear that she was volunteering for washing-up duties rather than actual cooking.

When they'd finished, he said, 'Shall we have our coffee in the living room?'

'That'd be nice. Is there anything I can do to help?'

'No, it's fine. But thank you for the offer.'

'Can I at least wash up?'

He shook his head. 'I have a dishwasher. No need.'

He did at least let her carry her own mug of coffee into the living room. It was very plain, with a sofa, a state-of-the-art audio-visual system, and a large bookcase. But there were masses of framed photographs on the mantelpiece, just as there were on her own.

'May I?' she asked, gesturing to the photographs.

'Sure.'

She put her mug down on the coffee table and went to take a closer look. There was a graduation photograph of him with an older couple who were clearly his parents, plus wedding and christening photographs.

'My brother, Riccardo, and sister-in-law, Helen, on their wedding day,' he said as she picked up the frames one by one, 'and with their daughter Emily on her christening day. And my sister, Chiara, and her husband, Mark, on their wedding day, and with their son Jack at his christening.'

They looked a warm, close family, she thought.

The photo she really liked was the family portrait of them all in front of a Christmas tree with an elderly golden retriever.

'That's such a gorgeous photo,' she said.

'My parents are at the stage of life where it's almost impossible to get them something for Christmas, so we get together and do a family portrait for them every year,' he explained.

'Including the dog.'

'Suki's part of the family,' he said simply. 'That's obviously last year's family photo. And actually it's lovely seeing Emily and Jack change every year, from babes in arms, to toddlers, to how they are now.'

Again, there was sudden sadness in his face, as if he was remembering something painful. She knew about his ex, but she was growing more and more convinced that he'd also lost a young child and that was why his ex had found consolation elsewhere— but she really didn't want to trample on a sore spot by asking him.

'It's lovely seeing children grow up,' she agreed instead. 'Lu gets an official portrait done of Ava every three months, and I've got all mine in a special album.'

'I have one of those, too,' he said. 'It's one of the perks of being an uncle—well, aunt, in your case.'

It was slightly more complicated, in her case. But she still hadn't found the right way to explain to him about Ava.

They curled up together on his sofa, just enjoying each other's company. But then Lorenzo stroked her cheek. 'Jenna.'

She turned to face him. 'Yes?'

He leaned forward and brushed his lips lightly against hers. Asking, rather than demanding; and she found herself kissing him back, sliding her arms round his neck and letting him deepen the kiss.

'I know this is maybe rushing things,' Lorenzo said, his voice low and husky, 'but you're irresistible—and right now I want to do more than just kiss you.'

Desire surged through her. 'I feel the same,' she admitted.

'Then maybe we should just go with our feelings,' he said softly.

This was it. Decision time. She knew if she said no, he'd give her space and take it more slowly.

But actually, she didn't want to take it

slowly any more. She wanted Lorenzo. All of him.

'That,' she said, 'is a very good idea.'

He smiled, and she let him draw her to her feet and lead her to his bedroom.

Afterwards, curled up in bed with him, she said, 'I guess I shouldn't overstay my welcome. I ought to head for home.'

'You don't have to go. Stay tonight, if you like.' He paused. 'Though I'm due at my parents' tomorrow. Every other Sunday we all gather there.'

So he was a real family man. That was reassuring. Danny hadn't been close to his family, and he hadn't been that keen on coming to Harris family gatherings, either.

'I know we said we'd take it slowly, but you'd be very welcome to come with me tomorrow,' he said.

She scoffed. 'That's not quite what your face is saying.'

He stole a kiss. 'I'm not doing you down. My family would adore you.'

'Mine would really like you, too,' she admitted. 'Lu's already asked me to bring you over for dinner.'

'It just feels too early to...' He tailed off.

'To let everyone else in just yet,' she finished. That was exactly how she felt. 'My family would interrogate you horribly.'

'Try growing up in an Italian family where everyone wants to know everything and there's this weird osmosis where you tell one person and then everyone seems to know it simultaneously,' he said. 'My family would interrogate you horribly, too.'

'So shall we just keep this between you and me, for now?' she asked.

'I think that would be a good idea.'

She nodded. 'I'll go home tonight.'

'You don't have to go,' he said, keeping his arms wrapped round her. 'This is comfortable.'

'But you're busy tomorrow—plus I need to be back at my place before nine so I can walk Charlie.'

He lifted one shoulder in a half-shrug. 'That's not a problem. We're both used to waking up early for work. And I have a washer-dryer, so I can put your clothes through the washing machine tonight.'

'Actually, I changed before I came out, so maybe if I can just wash my underwear and it'll dry overnight in your bathroom?' she suggested.

'That's fine. I'll show you where my laundry stuff is.' He stole another kiss. 'And I'll make us hot chocolate while you're sorting out your washing.'

Lorenzo really was lovely, she thought, warm and sweet and kind. So very different from Danny, thinking of others instead of putting himself first, middle and last.

But she still hadn't told Lorenzo the truth about Ava.

She really had to find the right words. And soon.

The next morning, Jenna woke to find Lorenzo curled round her. It made her feel warm and safe and cherished, and part of her wanted to stay right where she was for the rest of the day. But that wasn't the deal. He needed to go to see his family, and she needed to get up and walk Charlie for Evelyn.

She wriggled round to face him and woke him with a kiss. 'Good morning,' she said softly.

'Good morning.' He stroked her face. 'I'm glad you stayed.'

'Me, too.'

'What's the time?' he asked.

'Half-past seven.'

'And you have to go right now?'

She nodded. 'Sorry.'

He kissed the tip of her nose. 'Help yourself to whatever you need in the bathroom. There are fresh towels in the airing cupboard. And I'll make coffee and breakfast.'

'You really don't have to make me breakfast.'

He raised an eyebrow. 'You're seriously turning down a bacon sandwich and good coffee, on a Sunday morning?'

'Ah. In that case, thank you, I'll happily stay for breakfast,' she said with a smile.

Her underwear had dried overnight; she showered and dressed swiftly.

'Perfect timing,' Lorenzo said, and handed her a plate holding what turned to be the best bacon sandwich she'd ever eaten in her life.

'Thank you, this is fabulous.'

'My pleasure.'

He wouldn't let her do the washing up. 'It's fine. It'll go in the dishwasher. Besides, if you're late, Evelyn will worry about you, and that isn't fair.'

'That's true. Thank you.'

'I'll see you at work tomorrow,' he said, and kissed her lightly.

'Enjoy your family day,' she said.

'Enjoy your day, too.'

CHAPTER SIX

ON FRIDAY NIGHT, Lorenzo stayed over at Jenna's and joined her in taking Charlie for a walk on Saturday morning.

'He's gorgeous. A big fluffy teddy bear of a dog,' he said, ruffling the dog's fur.

'He's a cockapoo—a cross between a cocker spaniel and a poodle,' Jenna explained. 'And he's got such a sweet nature. I think he'd make a fabulous therapy dog, but obviously Evelyn wouldn't be able to manage taking him round to schools or nursing homes or what have you.'

Charlie was on his best behaviour, walking nicely beside them rather than pulling, and sitting nicely while waiting for Jenna and Lorenzo to throw the tennis ball for him in turn.

'He's a great dog,' Lorenzo said.

'Have you ever thought about having a dog of your own?' she asked.

He shook his head. 'Not with the hours I work. I'd have to leave the dog home alone for too long.'

'Me, too,' she said. 'I grew up with dogs, so I miss having one around and it's nice to be able to help Evelyn with him.'

With Georgia working part time, Lorenzo had thought about getting a dog. His family had always had a dog while he was growing up and he had wanted the same opportunities for Florence. Especially as Florence had always made a beeline for Suki, his parents' golden retriever, whenever they had been at his parents' house. He'd been about to suggest it when Georgia had dropped the bombshell about Florence not being his, and that she was leaving him to make a new life with Florence's natural father.

She'd moved away and left him to pick up the pieces of his own life—selling the house, which had taken months and months, and giving Georgia her share through his lawyer; sorting out all the paperwork for the divorce; facing all the pity and the conversations that stopped suddenly when he walked into the staff kitchen at work; and seeing the sorrow in his mother's eyes every time she looked at him, because she clearly realised how deeply all this had hurt him and hated the fact she couldn't fix it for him.

Lorenzo had struggled on for more than a year. He'd actually been at the point of asking his parents if they'd look after a dog for him during the day, because going back to that empty house with all the memories had made him so lonely and miserable. And then finally the house had sold and then the job had come up at Muswell Hill Memorial Hospital. The same job he'd always loved, but with new colleagues who didn't know his past and wouldn't look at him with pity. He'd jumped at the chance.

He knew he ought to tell Jenna about Florence. He didn't think she was the pitying sort, but he didn't want to take the risk that it would change the way she saw him. He liked the fact that she saw him for himself.

'Let's play ball with him,' he said, and held his hand out for the tennis ball.

Once they'd tired Charlie out and had a cup of tea with Evelyn, they spent a lazy day together, enjoying the food stalls and choosing fresh produce for dinner at Borough Market.

'Would I be right in thinking that you don't have a griddle pan?' he asked.

Jenna just laughed. 'You're lucky I have even normal pans, let alone fancy ones. Are you quite sure I can't tempt you to a bowl of hand-poured granola with hand-chopped fruit and hand-spooned Greek yoghurt tonight?'

He laughed back, enjoying her sense of humour. 'So that'd be a no if I asked if you had specialist pasta cutters, too.'

She gestured to the stalls. 'That's what this place is for. So people don't have to buy flashy gadgets they use once and then the things sit gathering dust in their kitchen cupboards. It's much, much easier and quicker to buy ready-prepped food from someone who knows what they're doing with the gadgets.'

'Remind me not to buy you a spiraliser instead of a bunch of flowers,' he teased back. 'I'll bake the salmon tonight rather than grilling it, then. I could cook it with a pesto crust.'

'Are you quite sure you don't want to be an award-winning chef like your cousin?' she asked.

'I just like cooking,' he said. And it was good to cook for someone else, to share the pleasure of food rather than sit at a table with only a medical journal for company.

Sunday morning dawned bright and sunny.

'After we've walked Charlie,' Lorenzo said, 'how do you fancy going to the seaside?'

'That would be perfect,' Jenna said. 'It's ages since I've been for a paddle in the sea.'

Once they'd tired out the energetic cocka-poo, he drove them down to Brighton. It was a long while since Lorenzo had been to the seaside, too, and he'd even made excuses to avoid Italy for the last year or so, because being with his big, happy, extended family was too painful a reminder of what he'd lost. But the sunshine, the sound of the waves swishing across the pebbles on the beach, and the scent of salt and vinegar from the fish and chip stands brightened his mood.

Better still, he was with Jenna. Being with her felt like being bathed in sunshine.

'So are you a funfair person?' she asked.

He had been. Florence had laughed and clapped her hands as he'd taken her on the carousel, holding her safely in front of him on the painted wooden horse. 'Dada! Horsey!'

He'd loved taking her to the swings and slides at the park.

'Lorenzo?' she asked softly, squeezing his hand.

'I…' He took a deep breath. This would be good for him. It might exorcise a ghost, maybe. 'Let's give it a go.'

As if she'd guessed that he was finding this hard, she held his hand without comment, not pushing him to talk but making it clear she was there for him. They started at one end of the pier and did every single thrill ride until they were out at the other end.

'Better?' she asked softly.

'Better,' he confirmed, and kissed her. 'Thank you.'

'Any time.' But that wasn't pity in her eyes. It was sympathy. And he liked the fact that she hadn't pushed him and asked: that she was waiting until he was ready to explain. 'Fish and chips are on me.'

'I'll take you up on that.' He stole another kiss.

They were halfway to the nearest fish and chip shop when they heard a scream and saw a small child sprawled on the pavement next to a lamp-post. The mum looked worried and the baby in the pram started wailing.

'I'm a doctor. Can I do anything to help?' Jenna asked, going over to them.

'I...' The woman raked a hand through her hair.

'Cuddle the baby,' Jenna said, 'and we'll look after your little girl—we're both doctors. I'm Jenna and this is Lorenzo.'

'I'm Sally. And my daughter's Daisy.' Gratefully, Sally scooped up the baby and began rocking him against her shoulder.

'Daisy.' Jenna gently picked up the little girl. 'Where does it hurt, sweetheart?' she asked.

'I bumped my head,' the little girl sobbed. 'And my knee. I want Mummy.'

'Mummy's here,' Sally said. 'The nice lady's a doctor and she'll make you better.'

'Can I have a look at your bumped head?' Jenna asked.

The little girl gave a shy nod.

'You'll definitely have a bit of a bump there tomorrow,' Jenna said, and took a small first-aid kit from her bag. 'I'm going to wipe your knee and put a plaster on it. While I'm doing that, can you sing me a song?'

In response, Daisy sobbed.

'You can help me sing a song, if you like,' Lorenzo said. 'Do you know "Old MacDonald Had a Farm"?'

'Ye-es,' she said, sounding slightly doubtful.

'Let's sing it together, and you can choose what animals we sing about,' Lorenzo said.

Jenna gave him a grateful smile. While Lorenzo distracted the little girl with 'Old MacDonald'—getting her to do the animal noises and a very loud 'ee-I-ee-I-oh'—she cleaned up the cut and put a sticking plaster on it.

'It's a non-allergenic plaster,' she told Sally. 'As she had a bump on her head, I just want to check her pupils, if that's OK with you?'

At Sally's nod, she took a penlight from her bag. 'Daisy, your singing is beautiful. Can you keep singing with Lorenzo while I shine a little light in your eyes?'

'Yes,' Daisy said, this time sounding less unsure.

'Equal and reactive,' Jenna said when she'd checked Daisy's pupils. 'Which is a very good thing.'

'What's happened?' A man carrying wrapped

parcels from the fish and chip shop came hurrying over.

'Daddy!' Daisy said, and burst into tears.

'Daisy fell and bumped her head. These nice people are doctors—they're helping,' Sally said.

'Thank you,' he said. But then he looked worried as Sally's words sank in. 'Bumped her head? Do we need to take her to hospital?'

Jenna shook her head. 'Just keep an eye on her for now. Children often go to sleep after a bump on the head, but keep a check on her and make sure you can wake her. If you can't wake her, or say by the end of the afternoon she tells you she has a headache, she feels sick or she's still sleepy, take her straight in to the emergency department and tell them when she bumped her head and what her symptoms are.'

'Thank you,' Sally said, still rocking the baby, whose wailing had turned to soft, huffing sobs. 'Both of you. That was so kind of you to help.'

'It's what anyone would do,' Jenna said with a smile. 'Take care of yourself.'

'You're really good with children,' Lorenzo said as they walked on.

Jenna rolled her eyes. 'I hope so, or I'd be a bit rubbish at my job.'

'No, I mean you have that warmth about you. Kids respond to you.'

'They respond to you, too,' she said. 'And it's not just your packs of cards and terrible jokes.'

Tell her.

She hadn't been judgemental when he'd told her the bare bones about Georgia. And that definitely hadn't been pity in her eyes.

Could he tell her?

If he opened up to her, would it change things?

Stupid question. Of course it would change things. But maybe she could help him move on. It still wouldn't be closure, but Jenna would have a different perspective on the situation, not having been involved. She might help him see a way through.

'Let's go and sit down,' he said.

'Sure.' As if she guessed that he wanted to tell her something monumental, she didn't try to chatter; she simply held his hand and waited while he found a relatively quiet spot on the beach.

Tell her.

He took a deep breath. The words felt as if they would stick in his throat, but he forced them out. 'I used to be a dad.'

She didn't leap in with questions. But she held his hand very tightly, just letting him know that she was there.

He braved a glance. There was only concern for him in her face. Gentleness, warmth, kindness.

He stared at the sea. Now he'd made up his mind to talk, why wouldn't the words come?

'You don't have to talk if you don't want to,' she said. 'But, if it helps, I'm not going to judge you—and everything that you say to me will be strictly in confidence.'

Funny, he hadn't even considered that. He already knew that that Jenna wasn't a gossip. 'Thank you.' He was silent for what felt like minutes, though it was probably only a few seconds. And then he swallowed hard. 'I met Georgia at a party—she was a nurse in the emergency department at the London Victoria, where we both worked. We started dating, and I fell for her. She was funny and sweet and smart. We'd been together for about six months when she told me she was pregnant.' He continued staring out to sea. 'The baby wasn't planned, but it didn't matter. We were going to be a family. I loved her and thought that she loved me. I asked her to marry me and she said yes.'

Now he'd actually started talking, the words spilled out in a rush. 'What I didn't know was that Georgia had an on-again, off-again relationship with a guy she'd gone to school with. Scott had fallen in with a bad crowd in his teens and started taking cars for joyriding. He'd been in court for it a couple of times; but it went from there to petty theft and then burglary. He was caught and sent to prison for a few months. Georgia broke up with him because he broke his promise to her to go straight, and that was the night she met me. When he was released from prison, he asked to see her. She told him it was over, but I guess they had a moment for old times' sake. Because he thought it was over between them for good, in his eyes there wasn't any point in trying to go straight, so he ended up back with his old crowd. He was arrested for burglary and sent back to prison—this time for two years. And I suppose Georgia panicked when she realised she was pregnant.'

'Because she looked at the timing and

couldn't be sure if the baby was yours or his, and he would still be in prison when the baby was born?' Jenna guessed.

Lorenzo nodded. 'She talked it over with her family. They all liked me and they persuaded her I'd be a much better dad to the baby and a better partner for her than Scott would.' He grimaced. 'I should've seen all the clues and worked it out for myself, but I didn't. I just took everything she said at face value. She said she didn't want to get married until after the baby was born, because she didn't want to be pregnant in her wedding dress. I know it's sexist of me, but I put it down to pregnancy hormones.'

'It was a reasonable guess,' Jenna said.

He sighed. 'I didn't push her because I didn't want to pressurise her. I tried to be understanding. But, because we weren't married when she had Florence, she didn't put my name on Florence's birth certificate. She said it didn't feel right to do that when we weren't married, and she'd get it changed as soon as we got married—but then she just didn't get round to it. Again maybe I was sexist, but I assumed some of it was post-pregnancy hormones and some of it was because it just isn't that easy to adjust to having a baby. I talked to a colleague to see how I could make things better, in case she had post-natal depression.'

Jenna squeezed his hand. 'That's not sexist, it's thoughtful. Putting yourself in her shoes and actually considering that things might not be OK for her.'

'It didn't ever occur to me that there was someone else. That she snapped at me all the time because I wasn't the one she wanted around, and that made her feel guilty and snap at me even more. I tried to be a decent, supportive husband and a good father.' And that was the rub. Maybe he hadn't been a great husband, but he knew he'd been a good dad. 'I fell in love with Florence, the moment I first held her,' Lorenzo said softly. 'She was my little girl.' He looked away again. 'And then, when Florence was eighteen months old, Scott was released from prison. He came round, saying that his mum had told him about the baby and he'd worked out the dates and knew Florence was his. This time, he really would go straight, for his daughter's sake. He wanted to be a family with them.' He blew out a breath.

'Scott was the love of Georgia's life, and he

told her what she wanted to hear. To be honest, once I'd seen his picture, it was pretty obvious that Florence was Scott's daughter. They both had the same red hair and grey eyes—and you and I both know that dark hair and dark eyes are dominant, genetically speaking. I assumed that maybe red hair ran in Georgia's family, plus Georgia had grey eyes. But, the second I saw Scott, I could see that Florence was his.' His face tightened. 'Georgia did a DNA test without telling me, and the results proved beyond all doubt that Scott was Florence's father.'

'That's…' Jenna shook her head, as if unable to find the right words. 'I'm so sorry you had to go through that.'

'Me, too,' he said softly. 'I couldn't contest Georgia for custody, because my name had never been on Florence's birth certificate and she had absolute proof that Florence wasn't my child. Bringing her up as my daughter for eighteen months counted for nothing. Georgia and Scott moved away, and she said it would've been too confusing to keep me in Florence's life.'

'But so many blended families manage to deal with having more than one mother or father. Surely it wouldn't have been that difficult?' Jenna asked.

'That wasn't the way Georgia saw it.'

'Does Georgia at least let you know that Florence is OK?' Jenna asked. 'Does she send you photos, so you can see Florence growing up?'

'No. She insisted on a clean break as part of the divorce settlement.' And that was the bit that hurt the most. He could just about handle the fact that he hadn't been Mr Right for Georgia, that she'd cheated on him with the man she really loved, but losing his daughter felt like being flayed alive. 'I hope for Florence's sake that Scott really has turned his life around and he's a good father to her.' He raked a hand through his hair. 'I did go to see her parents, but they said Georgia was their daughter so they had to stand by her wishes and support her. Obviously that didn't help me, but I understand where they were coming from.' He grimaced. 'Short of hiring a private detective, I have no way of knowing how Florence is getting on.' And how he hated that. 'She'll be three in a few weeks' time. And I won't even be able to wish her a happy birthday.'

She squeezed his hand. 'That's hard. I'm so sorry.'

'I don't want pity, Jenna.'

'I'm not offering pity,' she said. 'I'm sad that you've been so hurt, and to be honest I'm pretty angry on your behalf that Georgia didn't try to find a better compromise. Why didn't she tell you when she did the pregnancy test that she'd met up with Scott again and she wasn't sure if the baby was his or yours?'

'Maybe she was scared that I'd walk away as soon as she told me she'd cheated on me, so she'd end up being alone and would find it hard to cope with the baby,' Lorenzo said with a sigh. 'When she realised she was pregnant, Scott had already been taken into custody and the evidence against him was watertight. And she didn't actually know whether the baby was mine.'

'It was a difficult situation for both of you.'

'I wouldn't have walked away from her. Yes, of course it hurt that she slept with her ex, but we could've got past that. I would've supported her. I'm not…'

'Not like my ex,' she supplied. 'You're one of the good guys. And I'm sorry you got hurt like that.'

He shrugged. 'I guess at least she didn't lie on the birth certificate.' But that was a very small consolation.

'I don't know what to say,' she said. 'There isn't anything I can do to make it better. But thank you for trusting me.'

'Thank you for listening.'

This time she wrapped her arms round him. 'This isn't out of pity. It's a hug, because sometimes that's better than words.'

He hugged her back. She was right. This was what he needed most at this precise moment.

They stayed there for a while, just holding each other, and then she said, 'I also have a very English answer for right this very second. A cup of tea.'

He couldn't help smiling. 'That,' he said, 'would be good.'

'With scones. Warm ones.'

'Jam or cream first?' he asked.

She spread her hands. 'I can never decide, so I split mine between the two.'

Funny how just being with her made his heart feel lighter. Her solution of a cream tea really did make him feel better. As did the fact she asked him to stay when he drove them home, that evening. If he'd gone back to his own place, he would have lain awake and brooded. Instead, he fell asleep in Jenna's arms, feeling lighter of spirit than he had since Georgia left. There would always be a Florence-shaped hole in his life. But right now Jenna had made him feel so much less alone.

CHAPTER SEVEN

'I TOLD YOU you were fussing over nothing, Mum,' Cameron said.

'Nope, she was dead right to bring you in to see us,' Jenna corrected the teenager. 'I'd much rather see you now than in three weeks' time when you're in major pain. And a parent's intuition should never be underestimated.'

'Mum *does* fuss, though,' he said in a stage whisper.

'I do,' Mrs Blake admitted. 'Probably more than the average mum, because he's my only one.'

'Actually, given all the mums I've met in my career, I'd say most mums worry just as much as you do—it's perfectly normal,' Jenna said with a smile. 'I can give you a leaflet on Henoch-Schönlein purpura if you like, so you don't have to think back to our conversation today and worry that you can't remember it all.'

'Yes, please,' Mrs Blake said. 'I don't want to miss any important signs if he gets worse.'

Cameron rolled his eyes. 'Mum, I'm going to get a drink from the vending machine. See you in reception.'

'He's hitting the independent years, then,' Jenna said as she signed into the computer system and printed off the leaflet.

'Tell me about it,' Mrs Blake said wryly. 'Everything I do or say is wrong.'

'For what it's worth, you did the right thing bringing him in. We know what's wrong; if he gets any worse we can give him the steroids to sort out the stomach pain, so he's not distracted in his exams.' She gestured to the computer. 'I'll just need to take you over to the office where we have the printer to grab this, if that's OK.'

'It's fine. And thank you for being so calm and reassuring.' Mrs Blake followed Jenna over to the offices in the department. 'Cam's right, though. I do fuss too much. We couldn't have children naturally, and we had to admit defeat after four cycles of IVF. Luckily a very, very kind woman acted as our surrogate, and because of her we have Cam. I still can't thank her enough for what she did for us.'

It was just what Jenna had done for her sister, so she understood completely from both sides of the situation—how her sister had felt as a woman who was desperate for a baby, and how she'd felt as a surrogate who'd really wanted to help make things better in someone else's world. She squeezed Mrs Blake's shoulder. 'Knowing that you love him to bits and worry about him would be enough thanks for your surrogate, believe me. You carry a baby for someone else because you know how much that child is wanted and just how much he or she will be loved.'

That sounded really personal, Lorenzo thought, looking up from the notes he was writing in the office next door to where Jenna was talking to her patient's mum.

Or maybe he was overthinking it. From what he knew about surrogacy, surrogate mothers tended to have children of their own already, and he knew Jenna was single and childless. Maybe she had a close friend who'd acted as a surrogate, so she was talking from her friend's perspective. Though asking her would make it sound as if he'd been deliberately listening in instead of catching the tail end of a conversation and being curious; he didn't want her to think he was snooping, so he left it.

But then the question of surrogate mothers came up in the staff kitchen, a couple of days later, when some of the staff were chatting about a programme they'd seen on the television, the night before.

'I can't believe that storyline on the soap last night about the surrogate mum,' Keely said. 'If Jenna's been watching it, she'll be frothing at the mouth.'

Why on earth would Jenna be upset by a soap storyline about surrogacy? Lorenzo wondered.

Then he remembered the conversation he'd partly overheard. Had he been right in guessing that maybe one of Jenna's closest friends had acted as a surrogate?

'That's so horrible, with those poor people having a legal fight with the surrogate to keep their baby, and they'd already paid her all that money,' Keely continued.

'What I hate about it is that it's nothing like real life,' Sanjeev, one of the junior doctors, said. 'In the UK, you can't pay someone to be a surrogate mum for you. You're only allowed to pay their expenses.'

'Exactly. You know what you're going into when you're a surrogate,' Keely said. 'You're prepared right from the start that you're carrying a baby for someone else, so they're obviously doing it for dramatic purposes.'

'But if you were desperate for a baby and you couldn't adopt, and you were thinking about finding a surrogate, watching that storyline would put you right off,' Laney added. 'You'd be worried sick that it'd all go wrong, when in real life the agencies are really careful about putting the right people together. I really wish these dramas would get their facts right instead of twisting them to suit the plot—and I know they put that notice up at the end of the show with a helpline number to call if you're affected by any of the events in the programme, but it's too late by then. They've already planted the doubts and given them time to fester.'

'The woman who gives birth is the legal parent, and she can't agree to a parental order until the baby's six weeks old,' Sanjeev said.

'Plus there are all sorts of conditions about getting a parental order in the first place.'

Lorenzo knew about parental orders first-hand. His lawyer had broken the bad news to him. 'You have to be in a stable long-term relationship, one of you has to be biologically related to the child, and the child has to be living with you.' None of which had applied to him where Florence was concerned, and he'd had no rights whatsoever. He hadn't even been able to ask for access, because Georgia had proved that Florence wasn't his biological daughter. Bringing her up for eighteen months and being there for her mother during her pregnancy counted for nothing in the court's eyes.

Even so, everyone here seemed really well versed in the legal side of surrogacy—much more so than in the paediatric department at his last hospital. It was the sort of thing that the maternity unit staff would be more likely to know more about, especially if there was a specialist IVF unit attached to the department; so why did the paediatric department here know so much about it? Did someone here in the department have first-hand experience, maybe?

And again, he wondered, why had Jenna's name in particular cropped up?

Did it have anything to do with the sabbatical she'd mentioned, but never actually said what she'd done on her time away from her job? And Jenna had said that her ex had disapproved of a decision she'd made. Would that have been the decision to act as someone's surrogate and have a baby for them?

As a theory, it all hung together.

But she hadn't chosen to confide in him.

It was none of his business.

He should just leave it.

But it nagged at him for the rest of the week. That half-heard conversation with a patient's parent and the chatter in the ward kitchen... Perhaps he was adding two and two and making five. But somehow he didn't think he was. The answer he kept coming back to was that Jenna had had a surrogate baby.

The thought twisted deep in his gut, reminding him of how Georgia had lied to him about Florence. Why would Jenna not tell him about something like this?

Maybe he was being oversensitive and overreacting because it was getting so close to Florence's third birthday, and he knew from seeing his niece and nephew just how much he was missing out on; but it unsettled him enough for him to bring up the subject casually when he went out to dinner with Jenna on Saturday night.

'Keely and Sanjeev were talking about that soap storyline, the other day,' he said. 'The one about the surrogate mum.'

'Oh?' Her voice was perfectly neutral, as if he was talking about something as anodyne as the price of bananas.

Part of him knew he ought to change the subject. But part of him was hurt that he'd opened up to her and she was still completely closed off from him. Was she keeping a big secret from him, the way that Georgia had?

'Never mind. Forget I said anything.' He looked away.

Jenna had known for a while that she needed to tell Lorenzo about Ava. Especially because he'd told her about Florence.

But the words had stuck in her throat, along with the memory of how scathing Danny had been. And the accusation Danny had thrown at her when she'd refused to give in to his

ultimatum—untrue, unfair and totally un-
justified.

She didn't think that Lorenzo would take
the same approach. But what if he did? What
if she'd made the same mistake all over again?
She'd got Danny totally wrong. Who was to
say she hadn't got Lorenzo wrong, too?

But she couldn't put this off any more.
Not really. It was time to tell him. She took a
deep breath. 'You told me about Florence. So
I guess I ought to tell you about Ava.'

'Ava?' he asked. 'Your niece?'

She nodded. 'She's why I took that year's
sabbatical.' And now for the hard bit. 'I was
a surrogate mum for my sister, because she
couldn't have a child of her own.'

She was almost afraid to look into his face,
just in case she saw the same disapproval
she'd faced from Danny. But she made herself do it. She had to look twice, because she
wasn't quite sure what she was seeing.

'You took a year out of your life because
you were being your twin's surrogate mum?'
he asked. And then he said something she
wasn't expecting. 'That's the most amazing,
selfless thing I've ever heard.'

'You don't think I was stupid? Naive and…' The words choked her.

He reached across the table and squeezed her hand. 'No, I don't. That's the most incredible gift to give anyone—a child. Why would you think I'd judge you like th—?' He stopped. 'Your ex, right?'

She nodded. 'I know you're not him, but…'

'But, thanks to him, you've lost faith in your own judgement and you don't trust yourself or anyone else. I get that. Jenna, we all make mistakes—I've certainly made enough of them—but I'm telling you now that what you did for Lucy wasn't one of them. It was a brave, kind and selfless thing to do.' His fingers tightened round hers. 'You don't have to say anything more. You don't owe me any explanations.'

He didn't think the same way Danny had.

He actually approved of what she had done. He thought she'd done the right thing.

And that gave her the courage to carry on. 'I'm sorry. I shouldn't have judged you. Or expected you to react the same way Danny did.'

'It's fine. If it makes you feel any better,' he said, 'I was feeling worried that you might be keeping a secret from me, the way Georgia did. Though now I know with you it's the other way round—you were giving a baby, not taking one away.'

'I kind of understand why Georgia did what she did, even though I would have handled the situation very differently,' Jenna said. 'I would never have taken a baby away from anyone.'

'Wasn't it hard to hand the baby over, though, when she was born?' Lorenzo asked. 'You'd carried her for nine months. Bonded with her.'

'She was always Lucy's baby, not mine,' Jenna said. 'Yes, of course I felt that rush of love that you hear mums talking about when Ava was born. But I'm also a doctor. I knew what the hormones were doing to my body, and right from the start I thought of Ava as my sister's baby. She's my niece, and she's a joy to have in my life. I love being her aunt and spending time with her, seeing my sister's little girl growing up and exploring the world—and I see Lucy in her all the time.' Though she'd caught herself since feeling all wistful and wondering what it would be like to have a baby of her own and a partner to share that love with.

'So how come…?' Lorenzo stopped. 'Sorry. I don't mean to grill you. You don't owe me any answers.'

'And you're not judging me,' Jenna said.

'No. Not at all. Though I'll listen if you want to tell me. And everything you tell me,' he said, echoing what she'd said to him on the beach, 'will be strictly in confidence.'

She knew he'd chosen those words deliberately—to give her courage, the same way she'd tried to give him courage to talk. 'Can we… Just not here?' she asked.

'Sure. Go to the bathroom or something and I'll sort everything out here.'

'Sorry. I ruined dinner.' She bit her lip.

'You didn't ruin anything. It's fine. I'll make us an omelette or something back at mine if you want to eat later, or we can grab a kebab on the way somewhere.'

'Thank you.' She really appreciated how kind he was being. She would never have believed he could be so understanding about the situation. Though she knew it was wrong to let Danny's behaviour colour her judgement of all men.

She went to the bathroom and splashed water on her face, then joined Lorenzo by the reception area.

'Let's go,' he said, and took her hand.

They walked by the river until they found an empty bench, then sat down. Lorenzo simply waited until she was ready to talk, not pressuring her.

She took a deep breath. 'When we were twenty-seven, Lucy was in a serious car crash,' she began. 'She was driving up to York to spend the weekend with her best friend from university, having a fitting for her bridesmaid's dress—but she never got there. A lorry hit her on the motorway and her car was pretty much squished. She had serious internal injuries, with a ruptured womb—her ovaries were damaged, too, and they couldn't stop her bleeding in Theatre. It was a choice of giving her a hysterectomy or losing her completely. So obviously Will, as her next of kin, opted for hysterectomy. And we were all there, too, to support him—me, Mum and Dad.'

'A hysterectomy is a horrible thing to happen when you're that young,' Lorenzo said. 'It takes away a lot of your choices.'

Jenna nodded. 'Lucy and Will had planned to start trying for a family, the following summer. She was devastated, Renzo, when she realised that couldn't ever happen. But she got over the operation and recovered from her injuries, and then she and Will applied to be put on the register for adoption.' She grimaced. 'Except the authorities turned her down. Will's fifteen years older than Lucy, and the authorities decided that meant he was too old to be a dad.' She shook her head in disgust. 'I hate the fact that some faceless bureaucrat could take away their dreams like that, for such a ridiculous reason, because it was obvious to the rest of the world that Lucy and Will would both be brilliant parents.' Anger at the injustice flooded through her. 'Lucy and Will appealed against the decision but, even with the social worker's help, they lost the case.' She shrugged. 'So then it hit me. I was the one with the answer—I could be Lucy's surrogate and carry a baby for them.'

'That's an amazing thing to do for someone,' Lorenzo said. 'To give them their dreams.'

'She's my twin. She would've done the same for me.'

'It's still amazing.'

'It was an arrangement between me and Lucy, and we opted for IVF. The IVF team prefers surrogate mums to finish having their own family first, before they carry a baby for anyone else—because of course there are always risks with a pregnancy, and we didn't know whether I'd even be able to carry a baby to term. But we argued that we were a special case,' Jenna said. 'Because I'm Lucy's identical twin, this would mean we'd be having a baby who was genetically the same as her own would have been. The IVF team insisted that we had counselling first, but it was all fine. We used Will's sperm and my egg. Our family and friends were supportive—well, nearly all of them were.' She looked at him. 'The only problem was Danny, my ex.'

'Why didn't he want you to do it? Did he want you to have a baby with him first?'

'No. It wasn't that at all. He couldn't see that I was making the world all right again for Lucy.' Her lip curled. 'He saw it in terms of losing all my promotion prospects at work, the sheer cost of the IVF treatment—even though Lucy and Will paid for that, he still thought of it as money—and the amount of salary I'd be losing by taking a year's sabbatical.'

Lorenzo winced. 'That's an appalling way to look at things.'

'You're telling me. And, when I argued that none of that was important,' she said, 'he said he'd end things between us if I went ahead. I was so angry, I told him I didn't want to be with someone like him anyway.' Bile rose in her throat. 'Then he accused me of wanting Will and said this was the only way I'd get to have Will's baby.'

Lorenzo stared at her. 'You're kidding.'

'Sadly not.' She gave a hollow laugh. 'This was the man I'd actually been considering marrying. But I don't want to be with anyone who has no compassion and sees everything in terms of money, and who turns spiteful if you disagree with him. So I walked away.'

'Good. Because he sounds like a totally selfish idiot and he wasn't good enough for you.'

Jenna rather liked the fact that Lorenzo was fighting her corner. 'Thank you for— well, for understanding why I did it.'

'You're amazing.'

'I love my sister. And, as I said, Ava was

always hers. Lucy was there every step of the way, from holding my hand in the clinic when the eggs were harvested, and later when the embryos were transferred and during the thirty minute waiting time afterwards, through to taking the pregnancy test, every single scan, and the birth itself. Lucy was the first person to hold Ava after she was born, the person who cut the umbilical cord, the person who did the first feed with the milk that I'd expressed. As far as I'm concerned, she's Ava's mum—biologically, morally and legally.' She grimaced. 'I know it's a bit complicated, but they're my family and I love them. Ava's eighteen months old right now. When she's old enough to understand, we'll explain to her that her birth was a little bit complicated—but my egg was genetically identical to Lucy's, so her mum is still her mum and her dad is still her dad, and nothing has changed apart from the fact that her mum borrowed my womb so Ava could grow.'

'Eighteen months old. The same age Florence was when I last saw her.' His eyes were sad. 'It's a lovely age.'

'It is. She chatters a lot. And she loves dancing and messy play and making cookies—obviously the baking bit is with her mum rather than with me, but if I'm off duty I get to go swimming with her and Lucy, and it's just magical watching her grow up.' She smiled. 'And the best bit is seeing my twin so happy and fulfilled. With the life she always wanted—the life she deserves.'

Lorenzo put his arms round her. 'Someone very wise once said to me that sometimes this works better than words.'

'It does.' And knowing that this time she'd picked one of the good guys—one who was as far from Danny as you could get—was like a weight lifted from her shoulders. She held him close. 'So now you know.'

'And I'm sorry,' he said. 'I guess what happened with Georgia has made me a bit paranoid. I thought you were keeping some deep, dark secret.'

'I kind of was,' she said. 'And I'm sorry, too. I know you're nothing like Danny, but I was so scared you'd judge me. Especially because you lost Florence, and I didn't want you thinking that I'd just blithely had a baby and given her away. Ava was never mine to start with.' She smiled. 'I might be a tiny bit biased, but she is the most gorgeous niece.'

'You're not the first who hasn't wanted to tell me about a baby,' Lorenzo said. 'My little sister didn't want to tell me she's expecting—but I guessed when she was helping me clear up after Sunday lunch and she was gagging at the kitchen smells.' He grimaced. 'She didn't want to tell me because she felt as if she was rubbing it in. I told her not to be so daft—and I'd better be the first person she asks to babysit.'

Jenna pulled back slightly. 'Has anyone ever told you how nice you are?'

He laughed. 'You're nice, too. You're a hustler and you're bossy—but there's a sweetness about you. Not cloying and sickly, but lovely. You make the world feel as if it's certainly full of sunshine.'

'That's how you make me feel, too,' she said.

'That,' he said, 'sounds almost like a declaration of intent.'

She wasn't ready to say the three little words. But she was ready to think them. 'Maybe,' she said instead, 'you'd like to meet my sister? And actually you'd get to meet the whole family, because we're close and they'll refuse to be left out.'

'I'd like that,' he said. 'And maybe you'd like to meet my family, too. It's large, Italian and noisy—and close, like yours sounds.'

She nodded. 'Let's call them.'

'We'll call them now,' he said, 'and then we'll get some food.'

CHAPTER EIGHT

PREDICTABLY, BOTH FAMILIES jumped at the chance to meet. So, the following Saturday morning, Lorenzo met Jenna at her flat, carrying wine and flowers.

'You really don't need to bring anything just for lunch with my family,' she said.

'Yes, I do,' he corrected. But part of him felt ridiculously nervous. Would Jenna's family like him? In a way, meeting them would be like the most important job interview he'd ever had.

Once they'd taken Charlie for his run in the park, Lorenzo and Jenna caught the Tube to Lucy's house.

'Lucy's obviously my twin, this is Will, and Ava, my mum, Rosie, and my dad, Greg,' Jenna said, introducing them swiftly. 'Everyone, this is Lorenzo Conti.'

'Please call me Renzo. And it's lovely to

meet you,' Lorenzo said, shaking Will's and Greg's hands, kissing Rosie and Lucy on the cheek, and smiling at little Ava—who went all shy on him and clung to her father. 'Lucy, thank you so much for inviting me to lunch.' He handed her the flowers and wine.

'My pleasure—and thank you for these,' Lucy said, smiling back. She glanced at the label. 'Conti? Is that as in your family?'

'It's from my family's vineyard,' he explained.

'And Renzo helped pick the grapes for that particular vintage,' Jenna chimed in.

'That's impressive,' Lucy said. 'Come and help me put the flowers in water, and you can tell me how you like your coffee.'

In other words, he was in for a grilling. He glanced at Jenna, who just spread her hands and smiled. Well, if it was OK with her, it was OK with him.

'I know Jenna's told you about Ava,' Lucy said, when they were in the kitchen and she was putting the flowers in a vase.

'Your sister,' Lorenzo said, 'is an amazing woman.'

'I'm glad you realise how special she is.'

'I do, and I'm not Danny,' he said, though

he was pretty sure that Lucy would know her twin had told him about her ex.

'Danny!' Lucy grimaced. 'The less said about him, the better.'

'Agreed,' he said. 'And you obviously already know she's meeting my family tomorrow.'

'That means it's serious, for Jen.'

'And for me,' he said softly. 'I really want this to work.'

'Me, too. She deserves someone who'll be good to her.'

'That would be me,' he said. 'And I assume she told you everything about me?'

Lucy nodded. 'I'm sorry you've been through something so hard. Even the idea of not being able to see my daught—' She caught her breath. 'Well. Are you sure you're okay with Ava being around?'

'Apart from the fact that my entire working life is spent with children,' Lorenzo said, 'I have a niece and nephew I adore who are almost the same age as Florence. I've been looking forward to meeting Ava. But thank you for asking. I appreciate it.'

'It can't be easy for you. I know how bad it felt when I was told about the hysterectomy.

Will and I were planning to try for a baby, the following summer. And when the adoption people turned us down...'

He could see the tears sparkling in Lucy's eyes. 'But Jenna was there.'

'And she gave me the most precious gift of all.' She blinked the tears away.

'Let's change the subject to something that's not going to make you cry,' Lorenzo said. 'Something smells very good. What can I do to help?'

'Just tell me how you like your coffee.'

'White, no sugar, please.'

'That's easy—the same as the rest of us. I'll bring it out in a second. Now go and chat to the others.' Lucy shooed him out of the kitchen.

It was surprisingly easy to fit in with Jenna's family, Lorenzo found. He enjoyed talking history with Will and medicine with Greg and Rosie; and he could see for himself how close Jenna was to Ava. They clearly adored each other, as aunt and niece, and Jenna was right at the heart of her family. Jenna Harris was a woman who would never betray the man she loved or take his child away.

But there was still a tinge of sadness in his

heart. Jenna was very much part of Ava's life, whereas he was completely blocked out of Florence's. He shook himself mentally. Today was about getting to know her family, not fretting about his past.

Finally he ended up on the floor with Ava, helping her make a tower of bricks she could knock down and then patiently reading a series of board books she brought over to him from the lowest bookshelf.

'Ezzo 'tory,' Ava said imperiously for the fourth time, toddling over and thrusting another book at him. 'Ezzo 'tory, *peese*.'

'Hey, missy, he's already read you three stories. Enough, now. His coffee will get cold,' Lucy said.

'I really don't mind,' Lorenzo said with a smile. He'd always loved reading to Florence, his nephew Jack and his niece Emily; and he was charmed by the way Ava had pronounced his name when she'd asked for a story. *Ezzo*. His family would love that, too. 'I think your sister will tell you, on the ward, you take your coffee at whatever temperature you can get it.'

'I know, I know, it's a medic thing. Mum and Dad say the same. Even so.' Lucy scooped

Ava into her arms and kissed her. 'How about Daddy reads you the duck story? Then it's time for lunch.'

'Unch,' Ava said, and clapped her hands. 'Dada 'tory. Duck!'

'They're gorgeous at this age,' Lorenzo said. Ava was the same age Florence had been when he'd last seen her; and at the same stage, starting to put words together and making tiny sentences. He loved this and feeling part of the family, even at the same time as it squeezed his heart with a reminder of what he'd lost.

Lucy lived up to her reputation as a great cook, because lunch was fabulous—roast chicken with all the trimmings, followed by strawberries and home-made caramel ice cream.

'I didn't dare make lasagne for you, especially when Jenna told me that not only are you Italian, your cousin is a Michelin-starred chef who taught you to cook,' Lucy said. 'In fact, I was a bit worried about even cooking you roast chicken.'

He laughed. 'Apart from the fact that this was amazing—and, yes, I did notice that you put fresh tarragon and butter under the chicken skin—I have it on good authority that you make the best lasagne in the world, and I'm very much looking forward to sampling it.'

'Perhaps the next time we have a meal together,' Lucy said.

'The time after,' he corrected, 'because next time it's my turn to cook.'

'As long as it's that scallop and pasta thing,' Jenna said. 'It's amazing.'

Lorenzo couldn't help being amused. 'It does have a proper name, you know.'

'Scallop and pasta thing sounds good enough to me,' Lucy said with a grin. 'Be kind. Jen burns water, remember.'

'And offers people her special granola for dinner,' Lorenzo teased, and everyone laughed.

Will patiently helped Ava with her meal; and when they'd all finished eating Lorenzo shared the washing-up duties with Will before they all took Ava to the park.

Ava insisted on holding hands with Lorenzo and Jenna, and wanted Lorenzo to push her on the swings.

'You're a natural with children,' Lucy said.

And how he missed his little girl. 'I like kids.'

As if she'd guessed what he wasn't saying, Lucy said gently, 'Maybe when Florence is older she'll come looking for you.'

'If she does, I'll welcome her with open arms,' Lorenzo said. 'Biology has nothing to do with being a parent.'

'I'm glad you feel that way. Not everyone does.'

Lorenzo knew exactly what Lucy was telling him. 'Danny needs to take another look at his priorities.'

'Danny had better keep a million miles away from my sister, or I'll take him to pieces with a rusty spoon,' Lucy countered.

'I can assure you that you won't need a rusty spoon for me,' Lorenzo told her.

'Good.'

'Ava's adorable.'

Lucy grinned. 'I won't argue with that.'

'And so,' he said, 'is your sister.'

'I won't argue with that, either.' She patted his arm. 'I reckon you'll do, Renzo.'

'Glad to hear it.' He smiled, and continued pushing Ava until she'd had enough of the swings.

* * *

'I like him,' Rosie said, keeping her voice low, when they were back at the house and Will and Lorenzo were settling Ava in her cot for a nap.

'He's definitely a family man. And I notice he puts other people first. That's a good thing,' Greg agreed.

'Will said he likes him, too. So you can tell Renzo he has four yeses from us,' Lucy said with a grin.

Jenna rolled her eyes. 'This isn't a TV talent show, you know.'

'We know. But you knew we were going to check him out when you brought him to meet us. And he gets extra points for the way he played with Ava and read her those stories,' Lucy said. 'You picked the right one this time, Jen.'

'But I haven't met his family yet,' Jenna said. That could possibly be a sticking point. Bearing in mind how much Georgia had hurt him, no doubt they'd be very protective of him.

'They'll love you,' Rosie told her, patting her shoulder.

'They'll see the way you both look at each

other and they'll adore you,' Lucy added. 'Just as we noticed the way you look at each other.'

'We don't look at each other like anything,' Jenna protested.

'Oh, you do, love,' Rosie said gently. 'And that's a good thing.'

Later that evening, Lorenzo and Jenna walked back to her flat with their arms wrapped round each other.

'I like your family,' Lorenzo said. 'A lot.'

'Good. They liked you, too.' Jenna took a deep breath. 'One hurdle down, one to go.'

'You'll probably get a grilling from Chiara,' he warned.

'Like you did from Lucy?'

He smiled. 'That's what siblings are for. And I didn't mind. I knew she did it because she loves you and she's worried about you. Which is exactly why you won't mind getting a grilling from Chi.'

On Sunday, after they'd taken Charlie for a run in the park, Jenna picked up some fresh flowers to go with the chocolates she'd bought earlier in the week. 'I'm so not taking wine to a family who owns a vineyard,' she said.

'And, actually, maybe the flowers are a mistake, given that your sister is a florist.'

'No, it's not. Stop worrying.' Lorenzo kissed her. 'They'll love you.'

'Didn't you worry about meeting my family?'

He squeezed her hand. 'Of course I was worried. I wanted them to like me.'

'Exactly. And Italians are even more protective of their family than the English.'

'They'll know immediately that you're not like Georgia. They won't give you a hard time,' he reassured her, clearly working out what she was worried about.

Jenna wasn't so sure; but, when they arrived at Lorenzo's parents' house, the warmth of their welcome melted her worries away.

'Jenna, this is my mother, Luisa, and my father, Enrico,' Lorenzo said. 'My sister, Chiara, my brother-in-law, Mark, and their son, Jack; and my brother, Riccardo, my sister-in-law, Helen, and their daughter, Emily. Everyone, this is Jenna Harris.'

'Pleased to meet you,' she said, and handed the flowers and chocolates to Lorenzo's mum.

'How lovely—*grazie, bella*,' Luisa said, and hugged her.

'I didn't bring wine because—well, the vineyard, and Renzo absolutely hates the wine I buy,' she said. 'Sorry if that seems rude.'

'It's not rude at all, *bella*. You didn't have to bring anything, just yourself. Welcome to our house,' Enrico said, and hugged her warmly.

After that, Jenna lost track of who was saying what because everyone was talking at once, and she lost count of all the hugs, too.

The Contis were clearly a very tactile family. And she liked that.

'I'll put the flowers in water, Mamma,' Chiara said. 'Come with me, Jenna, and I can get you a glass of wine. The men can go and light the barbecue.'

In other words, Jenna thought, this was her turn to be grilled, just as her own sister had grilled Lorenzo yesterday.

'Good choice of blooms,' Chiara said as she put the flowers in water.

'Bringing flowers to a florist...' Jenna winced. 'I knew it was stupid. Sorry.'

'You brought the flowers to a florist's mother, if we're being picky. Mamma loves flowers, and I'm not in the least bit territorial,' Chiara said with a smile. 'Now, wine. Red, white, rosé?'

'Whatever's open,' Jenna said politely.

'*Chiaretto*, then.'

'The wine your family won an award for.'

'Lorenzo's told you a lot about us?' Chiara paused. 'Did he tell you…?'

'About Florence?' Jenna nodded. 'That was so hard for him. And I assume he's told you about Ava.'

'What you did for your sister was amazing,' Chiara said softly. 'The most precious gift you could ever give someone.'

'I love my sister and I was the one person who could make her world right.' Jenna shrugged. 'Anyone would've done the same in my shoes.'

'Not everyone.' Chiara looked closely at her. 'You have a good heart, and I think you'll be good for Renzo.'

'Just as I think he's good for me. So are you hoping for a girl, this time round?' Jenna asked.

Chiara's eyes widened. 'Renzo told you about the baby?'

Ouch. Jenna didn't want to drop Lorenzo

in it, so she fibbed slightly. 'Just that he was about to be an uncle again. But I remember what the early days are like. Plus I noticed you didn't have a glass of wine and Helen did.'

'Ah.' Chiara smiled. 'I couldn't *not* tell him about the baby, because I didn't want to leave him out. But I felt bad about the timing.'

'Because it's near Florence's birthday?' Jenna asked. Lorenzo hadn't actually said when it was, but she knew it was soon, and guessed that he'd find that day hard.

'Yes. We all miss her. And it's such a shame Georgia wouldn't let her daughter share our family. Jack and Emily are around the same age as Florence, and they all played so nicely together. We were good for her, and she was good for us.' Chiara sighed. 'But Georgia didn't see it that way, and she broke Renzo's heart.'

And Jenna hoped that she could mend it again.

'He looks happier than I've seen him in a long time. That's a good thing,' Chiara said. 'Now, let's join the others in the garden.'

The men were all fussing over the barbecue.

'They're all pretending to be Matteo,' Luisa said with a grin. 'Even Mark.'

Chiara rolled her eyes. 'Men and grilling things over a fire. It brings out the caveman in them.'

'Is there anything I can do to help?' Jenna asked.

'All the salads are done,' Helen said, 'and it's just a matter of putting the lemon and rosemary potatoes in the oven when Ric gives me the nod.'

'Let's leave them to it and play with the children,' Luisa suggested.

Jenna, used to being very hands-on with Ava, thoroughly enjoyed building a castle with Jack and Emily, taught them a song she'd learned the day she went with Lucy and Ava to toddler music class, and then sat reading a story to them with both children seated happily on her lap.

She glanced up to see Lorenzo looking down at her, a wistful expression on his face. Was he thinking of Florence? He barely mentioned her, but Jenna knew he was nearly always thinking of the little girl he'd lost. She wished she could do something practical to help, but Georgia was the only one who could change things. And even if Jenna by some means managed to contact her, she didn't think Georgia would listen.

'Everything OK?' she asked.

'Everything's fine. We're ready for lunch,' he said.

'We'll finish reading, and then we'll be there,' she promised, and duly finished reading the story.

The large trestle table in the middle of the garden was laden with bowls of salad, a plate with large slices of tomato interleaved with slices of mozzarella and avocado, chargrilled vegetables, grilled chicken, skewers of tuna and salmon that had been marinated in olive oil and herbs, and the lemon and rosemary potatoes Helen had mentioned earlier.

Jenna ended up sitting opposite Lorenzo and between the children. And how easy it was to feel part of this large, noisy family, she thought as she chatted with everyone, helped the children with their food and poured a glass of water for Chiara.

The meal was followed by grilled peaches, and the best tiramisu she'd ever eaten.

'Luisa is an excellent cook,' Enrico said,

'but you need to go to Verona. My nephew Matteo—now his food is really amazing.'

'Yes, Lorenzo, you must take Jenna to the vineyard and to see Nonno and Nonna,' Luisa added

Lorenzo spread his hands. 'There's the small matter of work, Mamma. We're both busy at the hospital.'

'You get annual leave,' Luisa said. 'And I know you're planning to go out there later in the summer. Make it sooner and take Jenna with you. There's plenty of room at the villa.'

Lorenzo looked helplessly at Jenna, and she smiled at him. 'I've heard a lot about the vineyard and Matteo's food,' she said.

'Then it's settled. I'll text Nonna now and tell her to expect you both,' Luisa said.

Later that evening, as they walked back to Lorenzo's flat from the tube station, he slid his arm round her shoulders. 'I'm sorry. My family's a bit full on.'

'I liked them,' Jenna said. 'A lot.'

'And they loved you. I had eight texts from them while we were on the train,' he said. *Eight.*

'Well, it's good that they approve.' She

grinned. 'My lot gave you four yeses. Five, if you include Ava.'

'That's good.' He wrinkled his nose. 'Eight texts. That includes one from Nonna, and one from Nonno, and they're not even good at texting! They want you to go out to Verona with me.' He looked awkward. 'I know my parents suggested it, but how would you feel about going to meet the rest of my family in Italy?'

'That'd be nice. I've never been to Verona or Lake Garda,' she said. But she remembered Lorenzo saying that it was his second home; clearly he loved the place.

'Maybe we could make a long weekend of it. Stay one night in Verona with dinner at Matteo's restaurant, one night at the vineyard, and one night just to ourselves by the lake?' he suggested.

'That sounds perfect,' she said. She stole a kiss. 'It sounds to me as if both our families think that this is a good idea—you and me, I mean.'

'So it's worth taking the risk.'

'It's worth taking the risk,' she agreed. 'Maybe we can sort out the off-duty rota tomorrow.'

'That,' he said, 'would save me from a gazillion nagging texts from my mum. And my sister. And Nonna.'

'Done,' she said with a smile.

CHAPTER NINE

A COUPLE OF weeks later, Lorenzo and Jenna headed for Verona. And, even though he was looking forward to their time away, part of him wished he'd chosen a different weekend. Florence would be three tomorrow—another birthday when he wouldn't have the chance to see her, or make a fuss of her, or even talk to her on the phone to wish her a lovely day.

But this was going to be a new start for him, a way of doing something positive on that day instead of brooding and missing his little girl. And he didn't want to spoil Jenna's trip. He wanted her to love Italy and love his family as much as he did.

So he forced himself to smile and chatter about Verona and Lake Garda on the plane. Plus he'd arranged to pick up a hire car at the airport that he knew he'd love driving, and hoped Jenna would find it fun, too.

* * *

Jenna stepped out of the plane at Verona and the heat hit her like a wall.

She stumbled slightly and Lorenzo asked, 'Are you OK?'

'Ye-es. I just wasn't expecting it to be quite this hot, quite this early in the day,' she admitted.

'Apparently there's a heatwave sweeping across the whole of Italy, so it's a good ten degrees hotter than it usually is at this time of year,' he said.

'Just as well I brought really light clothing,' she said with a smile. 'And I think we're going to need a lot of ice cream.'

He laughed. 'Great idea. Let's go and pick up the car.'

'Oh, now that's seriously flashy,' she said when she saw the bright red two-seater car, with its shiny wire wheels and soft top.

'This part of the world is made for cars like this, and today is the perfect day to have the roof down,' he said. 'Do you have a headscarf? Because you'll need to protect your head from the sun, and your floppy hat isn't going to work.'

'No, I don't.'

'That's easily fixed.' He shepherded her back to the shops in the airport and bought a headscarf for her. Once she was sitting in the passenger seat with the headscarf and her sunglasses in place, he smiled at her. 'You look like Grace Kelly.'

She laughed. 'Hardly, but thank you for the compliment. She's gorgeous.'

'So are you.'

'You're not so bad yourself, Dr Conti,' she said. But Jenna's heart gave a leap of excitement. She was happier with Lorenzo than she could ever remember. And being out here in the sunshine, with the roof of the car down and the wind in their faces and the gorgeous scenery, was just perfect.

He plugged his phone into the car and put on some bright, summery pop songs, then drove them away from the city and through narrow roads flanked by olive groves, lemon groves and rows of vines. It felt like being in the middle of a painting, and Jenna loved every second of it. Danny would've chosen a car like this because it was expensive; Lorenzo had clearly chosen it because he liked the design of the car and enjoyed driving it.

And that made all the difference for her: substance over style.

Lorenzo definitely had substance.

Finally he pulled on to a very long track; at the end was a massive villa.

'That's your grandparents' house?' Jenna asked.

'It's the family house,' Lorenzo explained. 'My aunts, uncles and cousins have apartments on the top two floors, and Nonna and Nonno have an apartment downstairs in the centre, along with the family rooms everyone uses.'

Nerves flooded through her, but she didn't have time to ask Lorenzo for any kind of reassurance because people were pulling out of the front door. Lots of people.

'Jenna, how lovely to meet you,' Lorenzo's grandmother said, greeting her with a hug.

'And you, Signora Conti.' Jenna diffidently handed her the flowers she'd bought at the airport that morning and the chocolates she'd bought in London. 'I, um… These are for you.'

'That's so kind! Thank you.' Nonna smiled. 'You're just like Luisa said you were. Now, you must call me Nonna, and this is Nonno.'

Jenna was introduced to so many people that she could barely remember everyone's name. But everyone welcomed her warmly, with a hug and a kiss on both cheeks, and she was swept into the kitchen.

'Coffee,' Nonna said decisively. 'And *torta di mela*. Apple cake. You'll have a big piece because you've been travelling, and travelling makes everyone hungry.'

Jenna glanced at Lorenzo, who spread his hands in resignation.

Go with it, then, she thought.

The coffee was excellent. And the cake... 'This has to be the best apple cake I've ever eaten,' she said. It was still warm, and the cinnamon and apple topping complemented the fluffy sponge base perfectly.

'I made it for you this morning,' Nonna said. 'With our own apples.'

After cake, Nonno showed her round the garden—including his prized roses—and part of the vineyard while Lorenzo stayed in his grandmother's kitchen for what looked like a serious chat, though Jenna wasn't sure what they were saying as the old lady had switched to Italian. She just hoped that she hadn't done or said anything to make the

Contis disapprove of her, because Nonna looked concerned.

'You must come back for the *vendemmia* in September—the harvest,' Nonno said when he took her back to the house.

To her relief, whatever Nonna and Lorenzo had been talking about while she and Nonno had been on a walkabout, they both looked relaxed now.

'It's hard work and a long day, but there's nothing more satisfying than picking the grapes when they're perfectly ripe and knowing that in years to come you're still going to enjoy the wine.'

'Lorenzo's introduced me to your award-winning wine,' Jenna said. 'And it's fabulous.'

Nonno looked pleased. 'My children and grandchildren are carrying on the family traditions. Though some have branched out. Enrico with his architecture and Renzo being a doctor.'

'And I get to meet Matteo tomorrow,' Jenna said. 'I've heard so much about his food.'

'He deserves that Michelin star.' Nonno smiled. 'And he'll be the first to tell you, he started learning in the kitchen at his grandmother's knee.'

'I remember teaching him how to tell when pasta is cooked, and how to make a simple tomato sauce of butter, tomatoes and onions,' Nonna said. 'He always wanted to know, why does this herb taste different from this herb, and what happens if you swap one ingredient for another. And he paid attention to how you present food to make it look as good as it tastes. I knew he'd go far.'

By the end of the afternoon, Jenna felt very much part of this warm, noisy, happy family; even more so in the evening, when she helped to set a massive table in the garden and carry large dishes of food to place in the centre, and everyone sat down to share bread, pasta, salad and wine. Lorenzo was right in the middle, the youngest members of the family were climbing over their Tio Renzo and chattering away to him, and he looked really happy. A family man.

Lorenzo loved having all the little ones chattering to him and wanting him to tell them jokes and stories, to see the drawings they'd made and hear all about their favourite cat or dog. But at the same time he was so aware of how much he missed his little girl. She'd be one of the youngest here, but she'd be right in the middle of them, chattering away and laughing and playing. So his happiness here was bittersweet; he was glad he'd brought Jenna to meet his family, but at the same time he couldn't help feeling how much Florence was missing out on.

Would the shadows ever go away?

Seeing Lorenzo here in Italy with his extended family made Jenna realise how much she'd fallen in love with him. Lorenzo Conti was a kind, gentle man with an enormous heart—a heart he'd kept guarded, though now he'd let her see exactly who he was and where he belonged. And she really wanted to be with him.

It was a real wrench to leave the villa, the next morning.

'Enjoy Verona, and tell Matteo we love him,' Nonno said, giving her a hug.

'And thank you, *cara mia*,' Nonna said, holding her close. 'Because of you, our Renzo is smiling again. That's so good to see.'

'Lorenzo's special,' Jenna said simply. 'And he's changed my life, too.'

'Good. Now, you promise me you'll come

back for the harvest, even if it's only for one day,' Nonna insisted.

'We will,' Jenna promised.

'And you remember what I said, Renzo,' Nonna added.

'*Sì*, Nonna.' He kissed her.

Whatever it was, Lorenzo hadn't chosen to share it with her, and Jenna didn't want to push the subject. Maybe it was her imagination, or were there shadows in Lorenzo's eyes again? But then he put on a pair of sunglasses and shepherded her to the soft-top car.

'Let's go,' he said.

When Lorenzo had driven them to Verona, on roads flanked by more vineyards and olive groves, it was still too early to check into the hotel, so they left their luggage in the hotel's store-room for later and went exploring.

'You took me to see the remains of a bath house in London,' Lorenzo said. 'Now I'm taking you to see the remains of the third biggest arena in Italy.'

And it was stunning: two storeys high with perfect arches outside, and massive pink and white marble tiered seats inside, along with a huge stage that was clearly set up for a production. 'This is amazing,' Jenna said. 'When I went to Rome as a student with my parents, I thought the Colosseum was incredible, but this... You really can imagine the audience sitting here and being entertained, because they still actually sit here in front of the stage.'

'We don't have time to come here tonight, because we have a table booked at Matteo's restaurant, but maybe we can come back to Verona another time and see the opera,' Lorenzo said.

'I'd really like that,' she said.

'And now,' he said, 'I have to take you to the most romantic place in Italy.'

He led her through the streets to an unassuming archway, which led into a small cobbled courtyard. Inside, the walls were completely covered with scribbles of names and labels and sticky notes and sticking plasters.

'This is La Casa di Giulietta,' he said. 'Juliet's house.'

She glanced up at the protecting rectangle built of brick and white stone. 'And the famous balcony, I presume—where Juliet declaimed "Oh, Romeo, Romeo, wherefore art thou, Romeo?"'

'The house itself is fourteenth century, but the authorities made the balcony from a seventeenth-century sarcophagus and installed it on the house less than a century ago,' he said with a grin. 'And obviously Juliet was fictional, but the house belonged to the Capello family, which is about as close as you can get to Capulet. It's still a nice thought, though. Celebrating love.'

Some of the courtyard was covered in ivy, and in one corner there were locks inscribed with lovers' initials. 'It's to seal their love,' Lorenzo told her. 'And if you put a note on the wall here, they say your love will last for ever.'

She shared a glance with him, and her heart felt as if it had done a somersault.

He hadn't said the three little words—and neither had she—but she was pretty sure that they both felt the same. That over the last few weeks they'd learned to trust each other, to trust themselves, and to trust to love again. There were still moments where she could sense the sadness in him, but maybe in time she'd help to heal that.

'Maybe we should follow the tradition,' Jenna said.

'We should,' he agreed, and took a pack of sticky notes and a pen from his pocket.

She blinked, not quite believing this. 'Are you telling me you came prepared?'

'Of course I came prepared.' He stole a kiss. 'And I've never done this with anyone else, not even Georgia. I never brought her to Verona.' He drew a heart shape on the sticky note, and wrote their initials inside it before handing the note to Jenna.

'Are we supposed to do this together?' she asked.

'We are indeed.' Ceremoniously, they each took a corner of the note and stuck it to the wall.

'And we have to do something else important,' he said, gesturing to the bronze statue of Juliet. 'Legend has it that if you touch the right breast of her statue, your love will last for life.'

Jenna could see that Juliet's right breast was much shinier and brighter than the rest of the statue. 'Then let's join the queue and do it,' she said.

'Do you want me to take your picture?' a

middle-aged woman standing behind them in the queue asked as they reached the front.

'Thank you—that's very kind,' Lorenzo said, handing his phone over.

They duly posed for the photograph with the statue, and thanked the kind tourist.

'So now it's just the last thing—the kiss on the balcony,' he said with a smile. 'Even though our families aren't like the Montagues and Capulets.'

'I'm very glad they're not,' Jenna said. They'd had a family barbecue, the previous weekend, and their families had got on really well. Ava had loved playing with Jack and Emily, toddling after them and letting Emily boss her about. All she'd talked about ever since was 'Emmy and Dak'. All three generations had liked each other, and Jenna had started to think that this was what she really wanted. A large, noisy, happy family.

And a child of her own.

But did Lorenzo want that, too?

The way he'd been with his family, right in the middle, made her think maybe he did. Now, among the crowd of tourists, wasn't really the right place to bring up the subject. But she'd talk to him later.

They wandered through the old house, looking at the exhibition, and then waited their turn to kiss on the famed balcony.

And he kissed her as if he really meant it. As if he was telling her without words, here in the most romantic place in Verona, that he loved her. That their love would last for all time, like that of the star-crossed lovers...

Jenna enjoyed wandering hand in hand with Lorenzo through Verona, exploring the city; the old buildings were beautiful, with the plaster on the walls painted all shades of cream, saffron, deep red, pink and apricot. Some had arched loggias; others had wrought iron balconies stuffed with terracotta pots of deep red geraniums which she couldn't resist photographing; and a tall stripy tower loomed up above the roofs in the old market place.

'This is so beautiful,' she said.

'There's something special about the city,' he agreed.

And when they finally went back to the hotel to shower and change, Jenna loved the view from the rooftop terrace: the red roofs of Verona spread out before them, with the sun setting in the background.

Nerves swooped in her stomach as they

walked to Matteo's restaurant. She'd got on well with Lorenzo's grandparents and his family at the villa. Would she get on as well with his famous chef cousin? Celebrity chefs always seemed to have volatile tempers which they lost easily; although Lorenzo had said that Matteo was down to earth—warm and sweet, like the rest of his family—she worried. Lorenzo was close to his family. If any of them didn't like her…

'OK?' Lorenzo asked, his fingers tightening round hers.

'OK,' she fibbed.

'It's fine. He and Patrizia will love you,' he said, as if guessing at her worries. 'Mum's already texted me to say that Nonna called her and told how much everyone loved you at the villa.'

Matteo's wife Patrizia greeted them at the door and showed them to their table. 'We're so glad to meet you, Jenna,' she said. 'Matteo will be out to see you with dessert and Alessia—our daughter—is your waitress tonight.'

'Thank you,' Jenna said. 'It's lovely to meet you, too. And the restaurant is gorgeous.' It was very plain, with soft wall lighting; the tables all had plain cream damask cloths and a single bright red gerbera, teamed with dark wood chairs with cream padded seats.

'Matteo wanted the customers' attention on the food, not the decor,' Patrizia said, following her gaze.

And how, Jenna thought when she tasted it. Lorenzo had ordered the tasting menu, so there was an *amuse-bouche* of a scallop in foamed anchovy butter, followed by courgette flowers stuffed with ricotta, taleggio and thyme.

'This is amazing,' she said when Alessia came to collect their plates. 'I can see exactly why your father has a Michelin star.'

The angel-hair pasta with butter and truffles was equally gorgeous, followed by cod with a sesame crust, spinach, creamed beans and wasabi mayonnaise.

And then finally Matteo came out to see them, bringing them the panna cotta with passion fruit.

'It's been too long, Renzo,' he said, enveloping Lorenzo in a bear hug. 'Welcome to Verona, Jenna. I hope you're enjoying our city.' He kissed her on both cheeks.

'Your food is utterly amazing,' she said.

He grinned. 'Thank you. Renzo says you

have a good palate but you're hopeless in the kitchen and even I couldn't teach you how to boil water.'

'That's about right,' she said, smiling back. 'Washing up I can do, though. Or pouring a bowl of cereal and mixing in some yogurt and berries.'

Matteo laughed and hugged her. 'Well, as long as you enjoy eating. That's what matters.'

'Oh, I do,' she said with a smile.

'See. I told you. Flashy dabs of sauce,' Lorenzo said, pointing to the plate.

'That's coulis, to you, Lorenzo Conti. Dabs, indeed. I'll have you know it's *artfully* done,' Matteo said, but he was laughing rather than appearing offended. 'How do you like the city, Jenna?'

'It's a beautiful place,' Jenna said.

'And yesterday you met Nonna, Nonno and the rest of the family?'

She nodded. 'At the vineyard.'

'It's a good place. Happy,' he said. 'I'm needed in the kitchen, but maybe Renzo will bring you back for a longer visit, next time, so Patrizia and I can spend some proper time with you.'

'I'd like that,' Jenna said.

'I will,' Lorenzo promised.

When they'd finished their coffee and petits fours, they said goodbye to Patrizia and Alessia, then walked along the river before finally heading back to the hotel. They sat on the wrought-iron chairs on the hotel's rooftop terrace, sipping Prosecco and chilling out under the stars. And when they finally went back to their room, Lorenzo made love to Jenna so tenderly that she thought her heart would burst with happiness.

'Thank you for bringing me here to meet your family,' she said. 'I know your parents pretty much pushed you into it.'

'That's par for the course in an Italian family,' he said. 'But their hearts were in the right place. They adored you and they wanted the rest of the family to meet you and adore you, too.'

'I like your family. And I like the fact that you're all so close.' She rested her head on his shoulder. 'I've been thinking. You know you asked me how hard it was to give up Ava, and I said to you it wasn't that difficult because I always knew she was Lucy's and I knew most of my feelings were due to pregnancy hormones? I don't think I was entirely honest with you—or with myself. I always did think of Ava as Lucy's baby rather than mine, and that hasn't changed; but now I know I want something like that for myself. A partner I love and who loves me all the way back, and a baby to make our family complete.'

Lorenzo had been thinking along similar lines, particularly when he and Jenna had stuck the note with their initials onto the wall at Juliet's house. But now she was actually saying it out loud, a rush of panic flooded through him.

Jenna wasn't like Georgia. She'd been open about the difficulties with her ex and he knew she'd been the one to walk away. He knew that Jenna would never, ever take a baby away from anyone. For pity's sake, she'd given her twin the most precious gift of all—she'd carried Ava for Lucy.

But the panic just wouldn't go away. The last time he'd committed to a family life, it was suddenly pulled out from beneath him.

And today was the toughest day of the year for him. Florence's birthday. He'd hoped that this year wouldn't be as bad as last year, that if he filled his time thoroughly and spent it with people he loved it would stop him brooding. Yet now it all slammed back. The loss. The sadness. The lack of closure. Not knowing how she was and if she was happy.

He wanted to move on, he really did. But today was the one day of the year he found really hard. A day when he didn't want to think about anything too monumental and taxing—something as massive as the idea of starting another family.

Everything was suddenly so overwhelming that he couldn't think straight and he couldn't think how to explain it.

He was silent for so long that she twisted round to look up at him. 'Lorenzo? Are you OK?'

'I… I can't do this,' he said. 'I'm sorry. I thought I could. But I can't.'

He hated himself for the surge of misery that welled up in her eyes.

'It's not you,' he said, wanting to make it better. 'It's me.' And he knew he owed her a proper explanation. He raked his hand through his hair. 'It's Florence's birthday today.'

* * *

Florence's birthday.

Lorenzo's little girl. The child he didn't get to see.

Maybe that was what his grandmother had talked to him about.

And Jenna had just talked to him about starting a family, on the day he'd clearly been upset about but had been trying to hide it. It was the worst possible time she could've chosen to talk about wanting children, and she wouldn't have said a word if she'd known what today was. She felt absolutely horrible, as if she'd just rubbed the top off all his scars—though she really hadn't intended to hurt him. 'Why didn't you tell me before?' she asked.

'Because I...' He shook his head, looking lost. 'I guess I wanted to try and do something positive today. I wanted you to have a good time here in Italy.'

'I did. But...' She bit her lip. 'You haven't.'

'It's not you. It's me,' he said.

And that was the problem, she realised. That hurt would never, ever go away. That aching sense of loss. She would always be part of Ava's life; but Lorenzo wasn't part of Florence's and never could be. And until he could come to terms with that—and she wasn't sure he ever could—he was just too hurt to be able to open his heart fully to someone else.

She simply wasn't going to be enough for him.

'I'm so sor—' he began.

'Please don't,' she said. 'Please don't say anything else, Lorenzo. I get it. I wish I could fix everything for you, but I can't. And I'm not going to make things worse by trying and failing over and over again.'

Jenna turned her back to him, lying right on the edge of the mattress, clearly putting as much distance as she could between them. How Lorenzo wanted to pull her into his arms and tell her he hadn't meant it like that. But he was pretty sure that she'd push him away physically, just as he'd pushed her away emotionally. Hating this whole situation and not having a clue how to fix it, he turned his back to her.

So much for this being the romantic weekend away he'd planned.

What the hell was wrong with him? His family adored her, and she adored them.

Why couldn't he break away from his past and move on properly, the way he wanted to?

He still didn't have an answer, the next morning. From the shadows under Jenna's eyes, she'd slept as badly as he had.

And things were more awkward between them this morning than he'd ever thought possible. She could barely look him in the eye.

'You have the shower first,' he said. 'Do you want me to arrange room service for breakfast?'

She shook her head. 'No, it's OK. I'm not hungry.'

'You need to eat, Jenna—or at least have some coffee,' he said.

'Coffee, then.'

He had pastries sent up as well. She crumbled a corner of one of them onto a plate but didn't eat. He didn't feel like eating, either, and the coffee didn't help much.

'I know we were supposed to be going to the lake today,' she said, 'but I'd rather not. I'm not feeling so great.'

And he knew why. Because he'd hurt her. 'I'm s—'

'Please don't, Renzo,' she cut in, and the pain in her voice slashed at him. 'I just want to go home.'

'OK. Give me half an hour to change our flights and sort everything out,' he said.

'Thank you. I'll go for a walk to clear my head,' she said. 'Alone.'

'But—'

'I'm a grown-up, Renzo. If I lose my way, I'll use the app on my phone to get my bearings and direct me back to the hotel.'

He couldn't argue with that. 'I'll see you later, then.'

What had she done wrong? Jenna wondered.

Or maybe it wasn't something she had or hadn't done. Maybe it was simply who she was.

Danny had rejected her, too.

She didn't think Lorenzo had rejected her because of the surrogacy; he'd seemed absolutely fine when he'd met her family. And he'd even said how much his family liked her. His grandparents wanted her to come back, his cousin had teased her but in a way that made her feel she was part of the family...

But Lorenzo himself clearly wasn't ready

for this. He might never be. She'd been the one to push it, last night. Buoyed by the way he'd looked at her at Juliet's house, the way he'd put a note with their initials on the wall, she'd told him straight out that she wanted a family. Too much, too soon; OK she hadn't known that it was Florence's birthday yesterday, but she'd known how much he missed his little girl and how hard he found it to let go of the past. She'd been carried away by the romance of the city, opened up to him about what was in her heart when maybe she should have waited. She'd fallen too hard and too fast for him—and this was the result. Utter misery.

Now she knew her mistake. And she'd keep things professional between them in future.

Lorenzo drove them to the airport, glad that having the roof of the car down meant it was too noisy to talk to each other. It was the best excuse he could come up with.

Jenna had completely backed off from him.

It was his own fault, and he knew it: he'd been the one to push her away. Then again, she knew his situation. If she'd really wanted to be with him, she wouldn't have let him push her away. So maybe taking things back to a professional relationship only was the best thing for both of them.

CHAPTER TEN

WORKING TOGETHER ON the ward was awful.

Lorenzo was perfectly polite and professional towards Jenna at the hospital; but she knew a whole other side of him, and she found it hard to reconcile the warm, sexy, gentle man she'd dated with the cool, closed-off doctor she worked with now.

She was pretty sure everyone else on the ward had noticed the coolness between them, though thankfully nobody seemed to be gossiping about them.

And of course Lucy had wanted to know how everything had gone in Verona, as had Jenna's parents. Jenna deliberately hadn't told them that she'd come back to London a day early, and because she wasn't supposed to be home on the Monday night she managed to avoid her usual dinner with Lucy on the grounds that she was in Italy. Being busy with work and her exercise classes during the rest of the week meant she'd got a breathing space until the weekend before she saw her family face to face, so she was able to fudge things and talk happily on the phone to them about how nice Lorenzo's grandparents were and how beautiful Verona and the area around it was.

She was telling them the truth: just not the whole truth.

The truth that she and Lorenzo weren't a couple any more.

The truth that she'd blown it.

She still hadn't found the words to explain to her family by the middle of the week, when she was rostered onto the Paediatric Assessment Unit. Thankfully, Lorenzo had ward rounds and clinic, so she knew she wouldn't have to work with him and face the awkwardness between them that day.

'Florence Reynolds?' Jenna asked.

A worried-looking woman stood up, carrying a toddler.

'Please come and sit down,' Jenna said, ushering her over to the cubicle. 'Obviously I've seen the note from your family doctor, but I always like to hear what my patients' parents have to say, so can you tell me how Florence has been, Mrs Reynolds?'

'She's always been healthy, apart from the odd cold that everyone gets. But a month ago she went off her food, started sleeping more than usual, and she seems to be breathing really fast.' She stroked the little girl's hair. 'I took her to our family doctor—he said he thought it was a bug, but she didn't get any better so I went back. He referred Florence for tests.'

'You said she's sleeping more than usual. I know she's only nineteen months old, but does she say she's tired, or do you just notice her getting more tired than usual when she does everyday things?'

'She doesn't seem to have as much energy at toddler group as she used to, and she seems to get out of breath quickly,' Mrs Reynolds said. 'We do one of those baby gym classes, and she's been a bit clingy with me there, wanting to sit on my lap rather than doing what the others do.'

Jenna made a note. Breathless, tired… 'Can I examine Florence?'

'Of course.'

Jenna noticed a slight dilation around Florence's ankles and abdomen. The little girl's pulse was slower than she would like; and the number of breaths Florence took per minute was more than average, too.

This was starting to look very much like a heart problem.

'I'm going to check the oxygen levels in her blood—what happens is that I put this little clip over her finger, and there's a beam of light to measure the oxygen levels,' Jenna explained. 'It won't hurt her.'

She wasn't happy with the oxygen saturation levels, either; and, when she listened with the stethoscope, Florence's heart sounded much too slow.

'I'm going to send Florence for a chest X-ray,' she said.

'You think there's a problem with her chest?' Mrs Reynolds asked.

'I think there might be a problem with her heart, but I want to do some more tests to be sure,' Jenna said. 'You can go with her to the X-ray department and be with her, and if you've got any questions at any point then please ask, because that's what we're all here for.'

When the chest X-ray results came in, they

really worried Jenna; Florence's heart looked big. Before seeing the Reynoldses again, she wanted a second opinion. But, when she went to find one of the senior doctors, of course the only one available *would* have to be Lorenzo.

Well, her patient came first. Even though she'd rather work with someone else, she'd just have to put her feelings aside and talk to him. Be professional and cool, the way he was with her. And she did at least respect him as a doctor. He was quick and knowledgeable; and he was kind to the patients and their parents, putting them at their ease so they could ask questions instead of looking things up on the Internet and worrying themselves even more.

She took a deep breath and rapped on his open door. 'Sorry to interrupt, but there isn't anyone else around. I need a second opinion on one of my patients, Florence.'

The colour drained from his face. 'Florence?'

Of course—she should have thought he'd react like that to the child's name. 'Don't worry, this isn't your Florence,' Jenna said. 'This is Florence Reynolds. She's nineteen months old, and I think she has cardiomyopathy.' Lorenzo seemed to shake himself mentally, and she ran through the symptoms. 'Can I show you the X-ray?'

He nodded, and she called up the file.

'I agree—it looks and sounds like a cardiac issue. OK. I'll come and see her,' he said.

She walked back to the cubicles with him—for once not talking on the way—called the Reynoldses in, and introduced Lorenzo to them.

'I agree with Dr Harris that we need to check the way Florence's heart is working,' Lorenzo said. 'I'd like to give Florence an ECG—it checks the electrical activity of the heart, and won't hurt her,' he explained.

The results backed up Jenna's suspicions.

'Dilated cardiomyopathy?' she asked Lorenzo.

He nodded. 'It's going to be a lot for Florence's mother to take in. I'll stay and back you up.'

'Thank you.' They might have personal issues, but Jenna respected his clinical judgement.

She called Mrs Reynolds in again.

'So did the ECG show what was wrong?' Mrs Reynolds asked.

'Yes. Florence has a condition called dilated cardiomyopathy,' Jenna said. 'It means her heart muscle has become enlarged and weakened, so it can't pump blood efficiently to her lungs and her body. That's why she's breathless and tired, and fluid has built up in her body.'

'But—how can that happen?' Mrs Reynolds asked. 'She's only nineteen months.'

'It can happen at any age,' Lorenzo said. 'Sometimes it's an inherited condition, or sometimes it develops after a virus.'

'She had a bug, a few weeks back—that's what our family doctor thought it was, but she just never seemed to get better.' Mrs Reynolds bit her lip. 'Can it be cured?'

'We can give her some medication to help with the tiredness and help her heart pump blood round her body a bit better, but because her heart beat is too slow she'll need a pacemaker as well,' Jenna said.

'What's a pacemaker?' Mrs Reynolds asked.

'It's a small metal box containing batteries and electronic circuits. It has wires which carry electrical impulses to Florence's heart to regulate her heartbeat,' Lorenzo explained.

'A metal box?' Mrs Reynolds looked horrified.

'It's not that big—it's about the size of a matchbox, and it weighs less than fifty grams,' Jenna reassured her. 'Because Florence is so small, you might see a raised bump on her skin where the pacemaker sits, but when she's older you won't know it's there.'

'It's programmed to a certain number of beats per minute, so if the gap between two of Florence's heartbeats is longer than it should be, the pacemaker will send an impulse through the wire into Florence's heart to make it contract and produce a beat,' Lorenzo added.

'And when the wire sends something into her heart, it doesn't hurt?' Mrs Reynolds asked.

'It doesn't hurt,' Jenna confirmed.

'But Florence will need an operation to insert the box into her chest,' Lorenzo said.

'An operation.' Mrs Reynolds looked petrified. 'But she's only nineteen months old.'

'If she doesn't have the pacemaker,' Jenna said gently, 'she won't get better and she might end up needing a heart transplant, which is a much bigger operation.'

Mrs Reynolds bit her lip. 'This is a lot to get my head round.'

'Of course it is, and of course you're worried.' Lorenzo squeezed her hand. 'But a pacemaker is the best way to help Florence get better.'

'Can you do the operation here?' Mrs Reynolds asked.

'Yes. We have a special operating room called a catheter lab, and one of the cardiac surgeons will do the operation,' Jenna told her. 'I'll book an appointment so you get to meet the cardiac team before the operation, and then after the operation we'll look after Florence here on the ward.'

'How long does the operation take?' Mrs Reynolds asked.

'About an hour. She'll need to come in the day before, so we can do tests to prepare her for the operation. She won't be able to have anything to eat or drink for about six hours before the operation, because she'll have a general anaesthetic—she'll be asleep during the operation,' Lorenzo explained. 'But you can stay with her right until she's had the anaesthetic and she's asleep.'

'Can't I go in with her?' Mrs Reynolds asked.

Jenna shook her head. 'We only allow doctors, nurses and technicians into the catheter lab, to help us stop any infections. But as soon as Florence is awake in the recovery room after the operation, you can be with her again.'

'But a metal box.' Mrs Reynolds looked anguished. 'You're going to cut her chest wide open?'

Lorenzo shook his head. 'The surgeon will make a small cut—not even as long as your thumb—under her collar bone on her left-hand side, so he can make a pocket for the pacemaker box and thread an electrode lead into a vein. He'll use an X-ray to help him put the lead in the right place in Florence's heart, then connect it to the box and fit it in the pocket.'

'They use dissolvable stitches when they close the cut,' Jenna said, 'so she won't have to have any stitches removed. And, when you see the surgeon, he'll show you what the pacemaker looks like and I think that'll reassure you.'

'Once she's awake again, she'll go back onto our ward, and the team here will check her wound dressing and give her antibiotics to make sure she doesn't get an infection,' Lorenzo said.

'Florence will have another X-ray, the next day, to make sure the pacemaker lead is in the right place,' Jenna said. 'We recommend she doesn't do any really active things like the toddler gym club for about three weeks after the operation, and during that time it's a good idea not to let her make big movements with her arm on the side where the pacemaker's fitted, to make sure the leads don't move.'

'Will it hurt, after the operation?' Mrs Reynolds asked.

'It might be a little bit sore,' Lorenzo said. 'We can give her some infant paracetamol to help with that, but it's important she doesn't pick at the wound or scratch it, or it might get infected.'

'And then after that she'll be better?' Mrs Reynolds asked.

'She should be better,' Jenna said, 'and she can live a normal life—though we would advise that you don't let her take up contact sports like karate.'

'The pacemaker will set off any alarm detector at the airport,' Lorenzo said, 'but we'll give you a card you can show to security staff. She won't be able to have an MRI scan with a pacemaker, and if you've got an induction hob in your kitchen she needs to stay away from it, because the magnets will interfere with the settings of her pacemaker.'

'And if she does look at things on your mobile phone, make sure the phone's in the opposite hand to where the pacemaker's fitted,' Jenna said.

'Will she have a pacemaker for the rest of her life, and will she need a different pacemaker when she's bigger?' Mrs Reynolds asked.

'To the first, we don't know—it depends how she responds to treatment. The pacemaker will last for about four or five years,' Jenna said, 'and then she'll need it to be replaced.'

'It's a lot to take in,' Lorenzo said. 'We can give you some leaflets about Florence's heart condition and about the pacemaker, and you'll probably have more questions over the next few days. Come and see us or give us a call, and we'll do our best to answer.'

'Thank you,' Mrs Reynolds said. 'I'm still trying to get my head round the fact she's so ill.'

'We can put you in touch with a support group, too,' Jenna said. 'It'll help to talk to other mums who've already been through this. But I would advise not reading too much on the Internet. You tend to get the really scary stuff there.'

'I guess it's like when you're pregnant,' Mrs Reynolds said, 'and you hear about all the really awful labours people have been through and not the ones that just went normally.'

'Pretty much,' Lorenzo said with a smile. 'Pacemakers have been around now for around fifty years, and about five hundred people in Britain get a pacemaker fitted every week.'

Mrs Reynolds looked surprised. 'As many as that?'

Jenna nodded. 'So our cardiac team is really used to doing the procedure. Florence will be in excellent hands.'

Mrs Reynolds blew out a breath. 'Thank you for that. I feel a bit better about it.'

Jenna smiled at her. 'We'll have Florence feeling better soon. And then you'll be less worried.'

'Jenna will sort everything out for you—

I'm afraid I'm due in clinic shortly and there are some things I need to do before I see my patients,' Lorenzo said.

'Thank you, Doctor,' Mrs Reynolds said.

'Yes—thank you, Dr Conti,' Jenna added.

'It's what I'm here for,' Lorenzo said, but his smile was solely directed towards Mrs Reynolds and her daughter. He didn't even look Jenna in the eye.

At least he too had put their patients first, she thought. And things would get easier between them on the ward. Eventually. It would just take a bit of time.

And as for how long it would take her to get over him...

She'd just have to focus on her job.

Lorenzo was checking through some files at his desk before clinic when his phone beeped. He took it out of his pocket and glanced at the screen; when he saw the notification, he nearly dropped the phone in shock.

Why would Georgia be emailing him?

And it looked as if there was an attachment to her email. Maybe it was a mistake, then, and someone had hacked into her account and sent a message to everyone who'd ever been in her contact list.

He went into his email account to delete the message unread, but accidentally clicked on the message.

When he saw the photograph attached to the file he caught his breath. It was a photograph of Florence, wearing a blue dress and holding a pink balloon bearing the slogan '3 Today' in glittery silver writing.

His little girl, on the birthday he'd missed.

He had to blink away the tears.

Why had Georgia sent this now?

The words of the email blurred before his eyes, and he had to read it three times before the message sank in. Georgia was moving back to London with Scott, who had a new job. They were happy; they'd got married and they'd had a little boy, a brother for Florence, the previous month. She realised she'd been unfair to him, so if he'd like to see Florence once they'd settled in he'd be very welcome to come round.

If he'd like to see Florence?

His heart felt as if it had just cracked.

She added the caveat, We probably need

to talk first and agree what we tell her about you. Maybe you could be her Uncle Renzo.

Not Dada. Not the man who'd held her when she was only a few seconds old, who'd brought her up as his little girl. That stung. But the important thing was that he'd still be part of her life: the thing he'd wanted so desperately and missed so much.

He looked at the photo again. Florence had changed so much in the last eighteen months; then again, he knew from his niece and nephew that toddlers changed very swiftly. He wondered if she'd become a total chatterbox, if she still loved having stories read to her, if she liked singing or dancing or messy play. Right now he didn't have a clue.

But what hadn't changed was the brightness of her smile. She looked happy.

And that was what he'd wanted to know more than anything: that his little girl was happy.

Once Jenna had booked the appointment for Mrs Reynolds and Florence with the cardiac team, reassured Mrs Reynolds further and given her all the information leaflets and information about support groups, she went in search of Lorenzo. Hopefully she'd catch him before his clinic and she could talk to him, thank him for his help and maybe try to bridge the gap between them. If nothing else, it would make things easier at work.

When she rapped on his door, he looked up. The expression on his face was slightly dazed. Was he OK?

He beckoned her in, and she closed the door behind her. Close up, she could see that he had wet eyes.

Something was definitely wrong.

'Right—start talking,' she said.

'I...' His voice tailed off and he shook his head.

For him to have tears in his eyes, something serious must have happened. Was someone in his family seriously ill—or, worse, had there been an accident? She couldn't just switch off her feelings or ignore it. He was clearly hurting and her first instinct was to make it better. 'Renzo, I know we're not exactly getting on right now, and you're the King of Clamming Up, but I do care about you and I'm here. Something's obviously happened, or your eyes wouldn't be wet.'

'Florence,' he said helplessly.

Oh, no. Worse than she'd thought. 'Something's happened to her?' she asked carefully.

'I… Oh, it'll be easier for you to see it yourself.' He handed her his phone with the email open.

She could see that the message was from Georgia, and there was a picture attached of a little girl that she assumed was Florence. On her third birthday, by the look of it. The day she and Lorenzo had been in Verona.

'Renzo, this is personal,' she said warily.

'Read it,' he said.

She scanned it swiftly, and she felt her eyes widen in surprise. 'She's actually going to let you see Florence?'

He nodded. 'I can't believe it, either. But it's there in black and white. She's even given me her new phone number so I can call her and arrange to meet.'

'What made her change her mind?'

'I have no idea. Maybe it's because they're coming back to London, and maybe her parents talked to her.' He shrugged. 'Maybe now they've had another baby, it's made Scott realise what they took from me and he's talked to her about it. But the main thing is she's actually going to let me see Florence.'

'That's good. I'm glad for you.'

He rubbed his eyes. 'Jenna, I have to go to clinic—it's not fair to my patients to be late—but maybe… Can we perhaps talk afterwards?'

'After our shift,' she said. 'Sure. I'll meet you at the main entrance.'

'Thank you.' He looked at her. 'Was there something you needed?'

Yes, but she wasn't going to ask and risk being rejected again. 'I just came to let you know that Florence Reynolds is booked in with the cardio team, and to say thanks for your help.'

'It's my job,' he said.

And their job was all they had together now. She got it. 'OK.'

'I'll see you later,' he said. 'We'll talk.'

Just as long as he didn't make it a Dear Jane talk. Then she'd have to stop him and walk away.

After his shift, Lorenzo waited by the main entrance to the hospital. And waited. And waited.

He glanced at his watch. He knew Jenna wasn't the sort to be deliberately late and he didn't think she'd just not turn up, so she was probably still with a patient. She was meticulous at work, kind and caring.

She was kind and caring outside work, too.

Even though they weren't getting on right now, she'd still noticed that something was wrong and still offered to let him talk to her, unload whatever was upsetting him.

Right now he had a lot to say. Starting with a massive apology. He just hoped that she'd listen to him and not shut him out—even though he knew he was being a massive hypocrite because he'd shut her out.

Eventually she came rushing up to him. 'Sorry, sorry. I was—'

'Patients come first,' he cut in gently. 'It's not like a job where you can close a file for the evening and come back to it tomorrow.'

'No. I just hoped you didn't think I'd...' She grimaced.

Just abandoned him? That wasn't Jenna. 'Of course I didn't. Thank you for meeting me.' He took a deep breath. 'Shall we go somewhere a bit quieter?'

'Good idea.'

They headed out to Alexandra Park, and found a quiet bench in a corner.

'First of all,' he said, 'I owe you a massive apology for what happened in Verona. I know I hurt you, and I'm sorry for that. That really wasn't my intention.'

She winced. 'It was my own fault. I expected too much. I shouldn't have said anything.'

He shook his head. Of course it wasn't her fault, and of course she hadn't expected too much. 'It's not that at all.' He grimaced. 'I should've told you it was Florence's birthday before we went. Actually, I probably should've arranged our weekend away for another date, one where my head wouldn't have been in the wrong place. Stupidly, I thought that being with you and my family, and keeping myself busy, would mean I wouldn't brood about not seeing my little girl on her birthday for the second year running—and I was wrong.'

'I wouldn't have said what I did if I'd known it was her birthday,' Jenna said. 'I know it's hard for you to deal with what happened.'

He nodded. 'I find it hard to talk about Florence, about what a black hole it was when Georgia left. I could just about accept that she loved Scott so much, it overtook her feelings for me, and that was why she cheated on me. That hurt, but I came to terms with it. But I couldn't accept not having my family any more. Not being a dad, when I'd loved it so much. And when you talked about having a family, all I could think about was how it felt to have that all ripped away from me.'

'I'm not Georgia,' she said softly.

'I know, and you'd never take a child away from someone. I know you're not like that. You've got a huge, huge heart and you're an amazing woman.'

'But I'm not the woman for you. It's OK. You don't have to say any more. I get it.' Her face was filled with sadness. 'I hope you find the right one for you, Renzo, because I'd hate you to spend the rest of your life feeling lonely. Even though Georgia said in that email she'd let you see Florence, she also made it clear that Florence isn't your daughter—that maybe you'll be like an uncle or a godfather or something, but Florence already has a dad and she doesn't need another one.'

Hard words, but he knew he needed to hear them. And he also knew that Jenna was right. 'All I wanted to know is that she's happy, that Scott's being a good dad to her and bringing

her up with as much love as I did,' he said.
'And you're right. I'm not Florence's dad.
Maybe one day she'll know that I was her
dad for a little while, while Scott wasn't there.
But just knowing she's happy, seeing her from
time to time—that'll be enough for me. And
I realise now that's what's been missing from
my life. What's kept me stuck and unable to
move on with anyone else.'

'OK. Well, if you want some moral support
when you meet up with Georgia, you know
where to find me.'

He was amazed at how generous she was
being. 'You'd do that for me, even though I
pushed you away?' Even though she thought
he'd rejected her?

'Of course.'

'It's like I said. You've got a huge, huge
heart and you're an amazing woman.'

She sighed. 'You don't have to over-egg
it, Renzo.'

'I'm not. I'm trying to tell you that you're
wrong about something.'

She frowned. 'What?'

'About you not being the right one for me.
I meant what we did in Verona. Before I was
really stupid in the evening, I mean,' he said.

'When we put our names on the wall of Juliet's house and we kissed on the balcony.' He hadn't actually said the three little words, but he'd made it as clear as it could be.

'But then you rejected me.'

And the pain in her eyes made him suddenly realise. It wasn't just that he'd backed away; it was that he'd backed away from *her*. 'I'm not Danny. I'm not rejecting you because you don't meet some ridiculous notion of what my partner ought to be.'

'You rejected me,' she repeated.

'No. It wasn't you. I panicked. And I couldn't find the right words to explain what was wrong and why I was being such an idiot. You'd think that, growing up in a massive Italian family where everyone talks a lot, I'd be good at that sort of thing—but I'm not. After Georgia, I went kind of inward on myself and stopped knowing how to talk about my feelings. I spent all the time smiling and telling everyone I was absolutely fine, when actually I wasn't.'

He reached over and took her hand. 'I should've told you that, although I was finding it hard to get my head round it, what you said you wanted was exactly what I want, too.

And now I know that Florence is happy, that I can see her from time to time, it's released me from being stuck in one place. Given me closure. And now I can move forward and I know what I want. A partner I love, one who loves me all the way back, and a baby to make our family complete. I admit it scares me, even though I know it's what I want, because I've been there before and it went wrong— and I don't want it to go wrong with you.'

'It went wrong for me, too,' she said. 'Not the baby part—I don't ever regret having Ava for my sister and I never will.' She lifted her chin. 'But I understand where you're coming from about telling everyone you were OK when you weren't.'

'Because you did it, too?' he guessed.

She nodded.

'I'm not Danny,' he said. 'I'm proud of you. Your priorities are in exactly the right place. And I know you're not Georgia.'

'But how do I know you're not going to close off to me in future?' she asked. 'That next time you're upset about something, instead of talking it over with me you're going to brood and push me away?'

It was a fair question, and she deserved an

honest answer. 'Because,' he said, 'it's different now. My head isn't in the same place that it was when we were in Verona. I've really missed being with you, and I've been miserable without you.' Right now, he could see in her expression that she felt vulnerable. So maybe he needed to take a risk. Say the words. Show her that he meant it. 'I love you, Jenna, and with you the world's a much better place. It's a place where I want to make a family. Where I can see us growing old together, watching our children grow up, and then having our home filled with grandchildren. Though I'll be the one making cakes in the kitchen, and you'll be the one teaching the little ones how to salsa.'

She looked at him, her blue eyes filled with worry. 'I love you, too, but it scares me.'

'I'm not going to let you down again,' he said. 'Before today, I didn't have closure, and that was what got in the way in Verona. Now things have changed. Georgia's actually going to let me be part of Florence's life. Not a huge part, but enough so I can see her grow up and know she's happy.' He looked at her. 'I want to be a family with you, Jenna. It'll be a blended family, but one full of love.' He paused. 'And I want a baby with you. Not a replacement for Florence, but someone for us both to love and help grow up.'

A partner she loved, one who loved her all the way back, and a baby to make their family complete. Everything that she'd seen make her sister so happy, and what she'd only recently realised was what she wanted, too.

'Be a family with you,' she said.

Her doubts still clearly showed on her face, because his fingers tightened round hers. 'I know this is a risk. I know that worries you. But I have your back, just as I know you have mine. So I'm going to ask you the question that makes me vulnerable, because I trust you and I know we can face anything together.' He shifted slightly so he could drop down on one knee, and took a deep breath. 'I love you, Jenna. I want to grow old with you and love you until my very last breath. Will you marry me?'

She could see the sincerity in his eyes. He knew this was a risk for her—just as it was a risk for him. But it was one he was prepared to take. Did she have the courage to join him?

He said he'd learned from the past. That shutting her out was a mistake.

So she could continue to put a wall between them in the hope of keeping her heart safe, and stay lonely; or she could give him the second chance he was asking for and look forward to the future—together.

And he'd said it first. That he loved her. And he loved her for herself, not for her position as a doctor or her salary. He'd said she was an amazing woman with a huge, huge heart—the same way she felt about him.

And that made the decision easy. She smiled. 'Yes.'

He whooped, pulled her to her feet, spun her round in a circle—and then kissed her until she was dizzy.

'I won't let you down,' he said when he finally broke the kiss. 'I love you. And even when life hits a sticky patch, we're going to be all right—because we have each other.'

EPILOGUE

Six months later

JENNA STOPPED TO catch her breath for a moment and grabbed a glass of water. Nearly everyone at the wedding was on the dance floor—their family, their colleagues, their friends outside work. The hospital band, Maybe Baby, was playing and really doing them proud. And the fast salsa she'd just done with her friends from her dance class had left her almost as breathless as her new husband did.

Lorenzo looked incredibly handsome in his wedding outfit. But, more importantly for Jenna, he looked relaxed and happy. And he was dancing with all the bridesmaids at once: his sister, her sister, Ava, Emily—and Florence.

'Look at them. They're all having such a

good time,' Georgia said, coming up to her. 'Thank you so much for asking Florence to be a bridesmaid. That's so kind of you—I don't have a sister and neither does Scott, so I never thought she'd have the chance to be a bridesmaid for anyone.'

'We wanted her, because she's part of our family,' Jenna said with a smile. At the slight worry in Georgia's eyes, she said, 'Families come in all shapes and sizes, nowadays. And I'm so glad you're able to let Renzo be part of Florence's life now.'

Georgia seemed to relax again. 'I panicked when we moved to Birmingham. I guess I was scared I might've made the wrong choice, and...' She looked over at Scott, who was rocking their little boy on his shoulder and talking to Will.

Jenna understood exactly where she was coming from: scared that Scott would go back to his old ways. It wasn't fear for herself, but fear for their daughter and that she'd chosen the wrong role model. But being a dad had clearly been the making of Scott.

'We all make mistakes and wrong choices,' Jenna said. 'But if we learn from them and we can get a chance to do it right second time round, like your Scott has—well, it makes life better.'

'You're amazing.' Georgia hugged her. 'I hope you and Renzo are really, really happy.'

Jenna hugged her back. 'Thank you. And I'm so glad you all came to the wedding today.'

'I wouldn't have missed it,' Georgia said. 'I know I hurt him really badly and I'm sorry for that. But he looks happy now. Thanks to you.'

'And to Florence. He's really enjoying being Uncle Renzo to her—and to baby Ollie.'

'That was Scott's idea,' Georgia said, confirming what Jenna knew Lorenzo had guessed a while back.

'And it was an excellent one,' Jenna said. 'Now go and dance with your husband, while I reclaim mine from the bridesmaids.'

She made a detour via the stage and asked Maybe Baby for a slow song; Keely gave her the thumbs-up. Then she walked over to Lorenzo. 'Might I have this dance, Dr Conti?'

'I'd be delighted, Dr Conti,' he said with a grin, and drew her into his arms. 'Happy?' he asked, holding her close.

She smiled. 'Very happy. You?'

'I've got a partner I love, and who loves me all the way back,' he said. 'Of course I'm happy. And I saw you just now with Georgia.'

'We were talking about Florence. And how families are all different shapes and sizes. You were right, by the way. The uncle bit was Scott's idea.'

'Just like I said—you have an enormous heart.'

She smiled. 'Funnily enough, so has my husband.' She paused. 'There was something that I wanted to talk to you about.'

She could see the faint worry in his eyes. 'Oh?' he asked carefully.

'What you just said. You missed something off the list.'

He went very still. 'Are you telling me...?'

'It's why I only had the tiniest sips of Prosecco during the toasts. I did a test yesterday morning. In secret—which isn't exactly easy when everyone's around helping with wedding preparations. Our mums, our sisters, our grandmothers, our aunts...' She smiled. 'I almost told you yesterday—but I thought today would be better.' Even though part of her worried, because this could be an opportunity for him to brood, the way he'd done in Verona. But hopefully he'd make the connection: Georgia hadn't wanted to get married while she was pregnant, but Jenna most definitely had.

'How long?'

'It's very early days. Six weeks, maybe. But we're going to have a baby, Lorenzo.'

She could see him doing the maths in his head. 'An Italian baby, conceived on the shores of Lake Garda on New Year's Eve.'

'The night we watched the sun set,' she said, 'and you showed me that mountain that looked like a face and told me that story about Lady Gardenia.'

'The immortal who fell in love with a mortal man, and when he died, she was so broken-hearted that she lay down and cried so much that her tears became the lake—Garda, which was named after her.'

'That's too sad a story to tell on our wedding day,' she said.

He kissed her again. 'Ah, but, unlike Lady Gardenia, we have a happy ending in front of us. A baby. And that's the best wedding present of all.'

And finally Jenna could relax, knowing

that Lorenzo had at last put his past behind him. And now they could really look forward to the future. As a family.

* * * * *

If you enjoyed this story, check out these other great reads from Kate Hardy

THEIR PREGNANCY GIFT
CHRISTMAS WITH HER DAREDEVIL DOC
MOMMY, NURSE...DUCHESS?
THE MIDWIFE'S PREGNANCY MIRACLE

All available now!